"We didn't not.

"What?" I sat down hard on the arm of the couch behind me.

"Are you okay?" Marc asked.

"No." I stood. "Yes. I'll be all right. Let me see."

She'd paused on a very clear shot of Pascarini, sitting upright, head bowed. The cop next to the professor pointed at her chest.

I squinted, not seeing anything. "What's he indicating? I don't see any blood." It would have been hard to tell on her dark jacket.

"We're not quite sure, but there's a spot of something here." Marc tapped the screen.

I saw what looked like a reflection a bit off-center on her chest. "How do you know she's dead?"

"She doesn't move, for starters. Her head is cocked at a weird angle. Also, after you drove off, Maya and I sat in the parking lot talking long enough to see other units pull up."

"Maybe she had a stroke?"

"They'd have been in a bigger hurry to get her to a hospital. We'd have seen an ambulance with sirens and EMTs rushing with a stretcher." He shook his head. "Nothing like that. No sense of urgency."

Good point.

"There's also this." Maya ran the video ahead and paused again, increasing zoom to show her cheek. "Looks like a bite mark to me."

"I think I understand why George isn't returning my calls."

That made two deaths on campus. But was it murder?

Also by Rena Leith

Murder Beach
Coastal Corpse

The Great Christmas Jelly Cookie Hunt
(Christmas Cookies series)

A Corpse for Christmas

by

Rena Leith

A Cass Peake Cozy Mystery, Book 3

A Corpse for Christmas

Cover Art by *Debbie Taylor*

The Wild Rose Press, Inc.
PO Box 708
Adams Basin, NY 14410-0708
Visit us at www.thewildrosepress.com

Publishing History
First Edition, 2021
Trade Paperback ISBN 978-1-5092-3917-7
Digital ISBN 978-1-5092-3918-4

Published in the United States of America

Dedication

For Eli

Chapter 1

Mia Howland, a slight platinum blonde, bounced on her toes in my living room. "They want to update the virtual tour of Clouston College's campus and make it more appealing to incoming students and their parents."

"You mean, a tour using virtual reality?" I asked.

"Sorry, no. By virtual, they mean not in person. Online. This will be enhanced. You can see their current tour by going to the college website and clicking on Take a Tour. They want us to use augmented reality. You don't need a bulky headset for that. Clouston's a small private school, and we've got a lot of competition from the Cal States and the UCs. We don't have the endowments they do, so we have to attract students with our uniqueness and our excellent location right on the ocean." She clapped her hands. "The Mavericks surfing competition is held right up the road."

I pondered the thought of stepping so far outside my comfort zone. We'd barely gotten CaRiMia, our website company, up and running. The upside of taking this job was that it provided us with a lot of visibility, but the downside of taking this job was that it was highly visible if we failed.

"I'm not sure I have the skill set to do an augmented reality virtual campus tour, although I did talk to a couple of former film students at the

Halloween party."

She nodded enthusiastically and looked over at her tall boyfriend, Ricardo Santiago. "Theda and Maya. Ricardo and I met them, and we could subcontract the filming. They might have access to high-end equipment, and maybe they need to do a project. We wouldn't need you to do the effects. I can do that bit, but you're good with words, so how about the script with your thoughts about where to add augmentation? If you look at the old tour, walk around campus with new eyes, see what you see, what seems cool to you, and then write it up, that'll give us a starting place. The augmented aspect will be fun!" She bounced again. "You can provide the older perspective. Y'know, like parents."

"Gee, thanks."

But I loved her enthusiasm. It had been years since I bounced like that. She had a point. I was at that age when I needed coffee to start my motor in the morning. I looked at Mia and Ricardo. The contrast between them could be startling. Mia was small and fine-boned with cropped platinum blonde hair and pale eyes that changed color depending on what she wore, whereas Ricardo was tall and muscular with long, black hair pulled into a ponytail at the nape of his neck and warm brown eyes. But although physically so different, they both were open-hearted, curious, and enthusiastic. And I really needed the money with tax season right around the corner.

"We could consider using drone footage," Ricardo said, his brown eyes crinkling at the corners. "The tour needs to grow organically. It's more money than we've made on any of our projects so far, and if we do a good job, there are plenty of other small colleges in the state that might be interested in hiring us. The learning curve will be big on the first one, but after that, we'll have the basics down, and the profit margin will be bigger. Besides, the campus is nearly deserted already. People are leaving for winter break, so it should be easy peasy."

"You just want to expense a drone."

"Oh, sure. Why not? What harm could it do?"

"Do you have time to go talk to them now?" Ricardo asked. "We're really going to have to move quickly to get the footage while the campus is deserted for the break. Do you know if Maya and Theda will even be here? Maybe they'll be visiting relatives for the holidays."

"Good point." I pulled out my phone. "Let's find out."

Maya answered on the second ring and confirmed that they'd both be around for the holidays and could come over now to discuss the project.

They were only five minutes up the road, so I took the opportunity to make a fresh pot of tea in my favorite ceramic tea pot painted all around with cats, all of whom looked friendlier than my overgrown black furball Thor.

Mia answered the knock on the door and let Maya and Theda in. After they'd hung up their coats on my antique hall tree, the five of us sat down around the old oak trestle table in my kitchen, sharing a platter of chocolate chip cookies still warm from the oven and the pot of fragrant white jasmine tea.

"I love it when the chips are all melty." Theda took a cookie from the platter.

"I know what you mean," Mia said. "These smell so delicious." She selected one and bit into it.

"Nothing like warm cookies and hot tea on a cold December afternoon. I added a little orange flavoring to perk the cookies up a bit."

I sipped my tea and gazed out the kitchen window at the choppy ocean. The wind was high this afternoon, turning the Pacific steel gray. A winter storm was moving in fast.

"I hope the weather holds if we're filming outdoors."

Maya looked out the window as she took a cookie from the platter. "Our friend Marc is the best videographer I know. I think he's also sticking around during the break. He might be talked into helping us if you provide him with some of these." She waved the cookie at me before taking a bite. "Thanks for having us over for your Halloween party, by the way. We're glad you moved in. This house has been empty for so long. Feels good to have someone living here. Hope you don't mind my walks on the beach."

"Your strolls along the beach are probably the most normal thing that happens out there. You'd be surprised by what I've gotten used to since I moved in. So, no problem. Drop by and say hi. I like to go for walks on the beach with Thor."

Theda's mismatched hazel eyes widened. "Your cat goes for walks? On sand? Near water?"

I nodded, smiling. Little did she know. "Thor is quite an exceptional cat."

Ricardo smiled. "That's an understatement."

Theda glanced over at my enormous black furball, lying as usual belly up. "He's…big."

"Oh, yeah. Bigger than a lot of dogs." I set my mug down. "We do have a small budget to pay Marc. Sorry it isn't more. We're doing some website work for the college in addition to the 360 augmented reality video tour that I hope you guys are going to be helping us with. Our business got started with community websites. We're branching out with this video tour."

Ricardo said, "The tour needs to look good on cell phone screens as well as on computers, tablets, and virtual reality devices. Will your friend be around over the break? Not going home to be with family?"

"We'll check, but I'm pretty sure he'll be here. He's fostering a couple of kittens. He's dedicated. He won't want to disrupt their training."

"Training?" I poured a bit more hot tea into my cup. "I didn't know you could train cats."

"It's not just litter box training. Play is only with toys. No hands. So, when they're adopted, they won't bite and scratch people, just scratching posts. Marc is also an actor, and he's part of a shoot in Santa Cruz," Maya said as if that explained everything and took another cookie.

"A *Method* actor." Theda raised an eyebrow. "When they're filming, he stays in character to keep the experience, y'know, authentic." She smirked at Maya.

"C'mon, Theda. Give him a break. Marlon Brando and James Dean were method actors, and you think they're great."

Theda rolled her eyes. "You'll see. He can be very angsty, Cass."

"Will that be a problem?" I frowned.

Ricardo leaned forward. "Is there a conflict with his acting job—"

"No, he's working hard to get a steady stream of jobs filming just about anything. Pays better than acting. All actors I know do something else to pay the bills. Don't listen to Theda." Maya cut in. "He's a complete sweetie. If he commits, he'll be there."

"He follows Maya around like a puppy," Theda said. "A really enormous, shaggy puppy."

"You're not making it better, Theda." Maya was about six inches taller than Theda and scowled down at her.

"I don't want to be the cause of a fight between you two." I maneuvered the plate of cookies between them.

Maya laughed. "You aren't. We argue about all kinds of techniques all the time. But Marc has the equipment, the know-how and will appreciate the work and the entry on his resumé. I'll go call him now." She started for the door and turned back. "Coming, Theda?"

"Not just yet. I'll be up in a minute." She picked her cup up to sip, watching Maya as she put on her coat.

Maya shrugged and left.

Ricardo and Mia stood. "Let us know when or if Marc agrees to do the filming. We really need to get a move on. Cass, you okay with working on the script?"

"Sure thing." I nodded.

"Okay then. We'll take off. Nice to see you again, Theda."

Theda set her cup down. "Looking forward to working with you." She waved as they headed for the door. After the door closed, she leaned forward on her elbows. "I'm going to swear you to secrecy."

I raised an eyebrow. "O-kay."

"I can't act. A media student who can't act!" Theda

slouched backward in the chair. "That's why I give Maya such a hard time about Marc. He really *can* act. He's damn good." She cocked her head to the left. "He is super tall and is pretty shaggy right now for the role. He has a shock of black hair. But he does become the character. Pretty amazing. Drives me crazy. And he truly is a nice guy."

"Why does it drive you crazy?" I was completely bewildered now.

"Because I can't do it. He makes it look easy. He kind of slides into the character." She sliced her hand sideways through the air. "The way he moves changes. Ugh! I'm fine in rehearsals when it's people I know, but point a camera at me…"

"Why don't you talk to him about it?" I poured more tea into her cup.

She clenched her teeth. "I can't now."

"Why not?" I frowned.

"We were in class together. The time to ask would have been then." She grimaced.

I wondered why she was telling me this. "You're playing games, you know."

"All media majors play games. It's what we do."

"Now you're generalizing. That's a defense mechanism."

I held my breath. My comfort level with these two was so high that maybe I'd taken this too far. Their help could be an essential part of this project, but more importantly, I genuinely liked them and didn't want to alienate either one. Quit overthinking. Relax. Breathe.

Theda glared at me. The old, familiar knot formed in my stomach. It happened every time I felt as though I'd messed up. A leftover from my ex-husband Phil's constant criticism. Oh, crap…

"Look—"

She closed her eyes and held up her hand. "No, you're right. I needed to tell someone. To see what it sounded like. To express." She rose. "My fear has gotten so bad."

I stood. "Theda, you can talk to me any time. I mean it. I know what it's like to be afraid, to feel the cold clamminess, to not know what to do. The only way to best the monster is to shine a big light on it, get it out in the open, laugh at it. And I know how that sounds, but it's true."

She nodded. "I know. I'll go apologize to Maya. You will like Marc. Guaranteed."

"You also need to talk to Marc. Seriously. Now I'm really looking forward to meeting him." I followed her to my front door and held it open for her.

She shivered. "Christmastime on the coast. At least we don't have snow."

"Not a skier? There's snow up in the Sierras."

She made a face. "I left Chicago to get away from winter."

I looked out at the white caps rising and falling in the choppy, dark water. "We have our own kind of winter here. Coastal winter is very different from the calmer, warmer Christmas in Pleasanton, too. There's a wild bleakness about the coast today." I smiled at her. "But hey, the sun's just sleepy this morning. Give it five minutes."

Theda laughed. "True." She walked across the porch of my little Arts and Crafts bungalow and down the steps, pausing to wave before she cut across the sand and grass expanse that passed for my yard and headed to her cottage up the road.

There was a lot to do. First, I had to write up the script for the virtual campus tour so that we could film it while the students were off-campus. Second, I needed to coordinate with Jack and Gillian about their plans to come to my place for Christmas. Third, we had to finish the Clouston College website. Fortunately, Ricardo and Mia were locals, so they'd be around over the holidays to work with me on Clouston's website.

I closed the storm door behind her but left the wooden door open. Thor stalked over and plunked down to stare out at the seagulls as he swished his long, black tail and chittered.

Doris, my resident ghost, joined us. "Not ready to tell her about me?"

"Not everyone needs to know about you."

Doris grew half a foot. "Really?"

I groaned. Who knew ghosts liked to socialize? "I like to ease people into it because some people— believe it or not—are afraid of ghosts."

She huffed. "Blatant prejudice against ghosts. What have we ever done to the living?"

"Scared the daylights out of us?" I ventured. "You gave me pee fright when you came through the bathroom door. You made Jack drop a beer."

"Pshaw! Minor damage." She raised her chin and made a sweeping motion with her right hand as if to brush away those minor details.

"Okay, what about the Bell Witch? Or Bloody Mary?"

"Ghost stories."

"The Vanishing Hitchhiker?"

"Urban legend."

I realized that I didn't know much about ghosts other than stories I'd heard or read, or seen in the movies. Doris hadn't been wildly forthcoming. All I could think of was the ghosts in movies. "Are you telling me there are no evil spirits?"

"I'd never say that." She laughed wickedly and vanished.

A chill trickled down my spine like a melting icicle.

"Doris! You're going to be the death of me!" I realized what I'd said and added under my breath, "Cancel, cancel, cancel!"

Chapter 2

That afternoon, I pulled out my laptop and started a new document in script format. After consulting the current tour on the college's website, I thought I understood the primary problem. Nothing in the existing tour would make a prospective student think it would be fun or enlightening to attend the school.

The campus was beautiful, but the video managed to make it look flat and uninteresting. The design of the tour was linear and sedate. There should be choices, giving the viewer the illusion of control. I made a note to add branches. Not my department technically, but I assumed Mia would figure out how to do the branching. As for the fun part, I'd hit up Mia and Ricardo for ideas to appeal to today's high school students contemplating college. I had to write it in such a way that all the paths would be logical and could loop back on themselves smoothly so that any path would seamlessly return to the main narrative.

I closed the laptop at midnight, satisfied that I had a solid draft. Physically walking around campus tomorrow would help me put it into perspective.

****

After my shower the next morning, I called Jack and put him on speaker as I mixed blueberries into my Greek yogurt. "Hey."

"You okay?" He yawned.

"Of course. Having breakfast. You?"

"Finishing up some work stuff before we drive over on Saturday. We have to be back at work on Monday the twenty-eighth."

"Glad to have you for a week. I'll lay in some supplies. A new distillery opened up with cocktails on tap. You'll love it. They even can them so that you can enjoy at home." I started a list on the notepad on the counter and doodled a can.

Jack laughed. "Looking forward to it. We'll call when we're on the way. We have a few goodies for you. Anything you want us to bring?"

"Just yourselves. Aside from working on the campus tour video, I expect this week to be quiet and cozy."

"See you soon!"

I disconnected the call and took a moment to check messages and email. Nothing but promos, holiday sales, and spam. I finished my yogurt and put my bowl in the sink, added some dry chicken and rice food to Thor's bowl, slipped on my jacket, and headed out to drive to campus to meet Theda, Maya, and Marc.

****

Parking had never been so easy on campus. The crisp air carried the scent of salt out here on the peninsula. A stiff breeze inspired me to zip my fleece up and hunch over as I pushed toward the fountain and reflecting pool in front of the administration building. The tall guy with the shaggy black hair setting up a tripod must be Marc. As I reached him, Maya hailed me as she headed up from the opposite direction.

At the sound of her voice, Marc turned, the wind riffling his hair. A crooked grin warmed his face, and affection crinkled his dark gray-green eyes. So Theda had been right about his interest in Maya. She got to him before I did, and he bent to hug her.

Maya was about my height and I'm five-foot eight. Marc made her look small. I estimated his height around six-three.

Maya rubbed his upper arm as she introduced us. "Marc, this is Cass Peake. She's the one hiring us."

He smiled, and we shook. His hand was strong and warm despite the weather and his lack of gloves. His nails were clean and short, which I wasn't expecting, given his long, unevenly cut hair. My jealousy bone twanged. That mane was glossy and thick. In fact, he was well-groomed except for the unevenness of the cut that gave him such a shaggy appearance.

"Thanks. I appreciate it," he said.

I returned his smile. "You're doing me a favor. I'm still not sure I understand augmented reality."

He shrugged. "It's really a matter of providing more info right where and when you need it. Instead of looking at a tour and then having to read or hear about it from another source, you get all the data rolled into one source, using pop-ups or voiceovers or animation—whatever you like."

"What do you think of the existing tour?"

He shrugged his right shoulder. "It's fine. Very polished."

"But?"

He looked at Maya, and she nodded. He turned back to me with a resigned sigh.

"It's very static. They might have done the same thing with still pictures in a brochure. We can populate the scene we're filming but with control." He gestured.

"A small group walking and talking over there. Someone studying under a tree. The scene needs to come alive. *Move*. Future students need to be able to picture themselves on campus and involved. We can use augmentation to provide history and architecture tidbits. Do we have access to the buildings?"

I nodded, thinking about what Ricardo had told me. "Robbie is our contact with the campus cops. We touch base and let him know what we want. He'll make sure we can get into whatever buildings we need. Student Union. Crabbers Club. Classrooms. Labs. Library. Administration. Dorms." I gestured toward the stately hall we stood in front of, stone lions and all. Classic. "So, the campus is deserted?" I glanced around at the serene gray limestone-clad buildings.

Marc shook his head. "Not entirely. I did some checking." He held up a finger. "One small complication. There's a reunion of the Black Triangle club on campus over the break. I believe there are 12 members, judging by old yearbooks."

Hmm. He'd done some research. I liked that.

"Never heard of them." Maya's brow furrowed.

"Not surprising. They were disbanded on campus years ago after the last member graduated. It wasn't a national club. It only existed at Clouston. Very private. I'm not sure what they did or even what they stood for. Invitation only. There were still vague whispers when I was a freshman," Marc said. "Some people believed that they had gone underground."

She frowned. "Wait a minute. I remember something. Wasn't there a black mass?" She shivered.

"It was the time for it." Marc placed his arm around her shoulders. "Rumor has it there was a private party, and somebody died. It was all hushed up. Secret society means everyone sworn to secrecy. Apparently, no one cracked because no one was charged with anything. The group met off campus a few times and then was ordered to disband by the administration. As far as anyone knew, that was the end of that."

"The reunion is an officially sanctioned event," I said. "So, I doubt that they were disbanded." But my curiosity was aroused.

"Good point. Not if they're having a reunion using campus facilities. Bit of a mystery then," Marc said. "But it is a fact that the club doesn't appear in yearbooks after the last known member graduated. I checked."

"More importantly," Maya said. "They won't get in our way, will they?"

He shrugged. "I doubt it. If they have events, we can shoot around them. The club was never very big."

"Twelve doesn't sound like too much of a threat," Maya said.

I pursed my lips. "I'm sure they won't be a problem."

"Hey!" We all turned at the harsh sound of the angry voice.

A small woman, dark hair pulled back in a bun and wearing a long, flowing black dress, advanced on us, waving a walking stick.

"Actress?" I wondered. "Is she in a costume?"

Marc shrugged. "No one I know."

She stopped abruptly in front of me, eyes blazing, and shook a finger two inches from my nose. "Who the hell do you think you are?"

I thought I detected an East Coast accent. My

various identities flashed through my brain: divorcée, sister, failure, success.

"Sanctioned by the college."

"Sanctioned to do what?"

Her clipped rudeness annoyed me.

"Film a tour."

"We'll see about that." She stalked off, muttering to herself as the staccato beat of her metal-tipped dark wood walking stick marked her progress toward the administration building.

It was as if someone released the pause button, and we all started talking at once.

"What the hell…?"

"Who was that?"

"Who does she think she is?"

I laughed out of nerves. "Marc, can you get a picture of her?"

He raised his camera and took several bursts in one smooth motion. "Even her backside speaks volumes."

I nodded. "Rigid. Tight. Hidebound. Dictatorial. And very, very selfish."

"Raised in a barn," Maya added.

"Yep. No manners." Marc went back to taking the shots he needed. When he finished, he straightened.

Again, his height struck me. I don't think of myself as short.

"Uh, shall I call Robbie now?"

"You shall." Marc's lopsided grin warmed his face and crinkled his eyes.

"While I walk on campus for exercise," I said. "I have no idea where some of these locations are."

Maya took the list from me. "No prob."

While she perused it, I called Robbie and put him

on speaker. "Hi, Robbie. This is Cass Peake. We're on campus now. If it works for you, could you let us into the buildings?"

"Where are you?"

"I'm with two former students. I'm sure they can find their way to whichever location you want to do first." I looked at Marc and Maya, who gave me a thumbs up.

"Let's start with the Crabber's Club," Robbie said.

"Crabber's Club?" I repeated, trying to look hopeful.

Marc nodded and mouthed, "Sure."

"Okay, we'll be there in a few minutes." I ended the call.

Marc picked up his gear and took the lead as we walked along the winding paths that cut through the carefully tended lawns to our rendezvous.

Robbie greeted us and let us in. Our destination looked like a normal campus building outside, but the little club tucked away on the first floor was filled with college and fishing kitsch, right down to nets hanging on the walls and mermaids suspended from the ceiling.

"Thanks, Robbie. This is quite the place." I spotted a replica of the famous fake mermaid baby with a scarf in the maroon and olive colors of Clouston College wrapped around its neck.

Robbie grunted.

Marc took a few shots with Maya posing. "This place has...possibilities." The corner of his mouth crooked up.

"Don't get too carried away. This virtual tour is supposed to entice students to come here but also appeal to their parents, who're most likely footing the bill." I turned to Robbie. "Student Union next?"

"Over here." He led the way down the tree-lined sidewalk between the two buildings. As we rounded the corner, the woman with the bun and walking stick headed our way. She hesitated, turned around, and hobbled away, leaning on her cane. I glanced at Robbie, who was staring after her, frowning.

"Do you know her?" I asked.

He bit his lip. "Yes, she's part of an alumni group that's staying on campus over the break. We've talked a few times. But why didn't she come over to say hi?"

"I don't think she's happy that we're filming here." I watched her retreating figure. "I thought the campus was deserted. We're supposed to be uninterrupted here while we make the new virtual tour. Where are they staying?"

"In the Delft dorm on the quad." He tucked his thumbs into his belt.

Out of the corner of my eye, I saw Marc and Maya exchange a glance. I included them in my question. "Where's that?"

Maya touched my arm. "We'll show you later."

"We'll need to shoot in one of those dorms for the tour," Marc said.

When we reached the door to the Student Union, Robbie pointed up. "Two of them are still here in the guest rooms: Sophia Pascarini, the woman you just saw, and Jonathan Alcott. Both have health issues that make this a better location for them. The rest have moved over to the dorm on the south side of campus." He gestured in that general direction.

"The woman with the cane is staying in the same building as the Student Union?"

This would be tricky, but at least she hadn't accosted us again. I figured she merely wanted to get to her room. Good to know.

"This building is accessible." Robbie opened the door, and we trooped in. "They have some limited service here over the break due to the guests."

"We'll have to plan shooting here very carefully. Avoid meal times." I glanced around.

We wandered through into the main entrance hall near the bank of elevators. "Get shots of the green granite and the sweep of the windows. We have to do something with that."

Marc kept shooting, occasionally switching cameras or lenses.

"There's a gym in the building. Exclusive for guests and admin."

"I thought there was a new gym facility closer to the point," Maya said.

"There is, with a padded indoor track. The gym here is old-style. Unique. I don't know if you want to include that, given it's not used by students."

Marc paused, holding the camera down by his side, the straps dangling.

I thought for a moment. "Can we have a look, Robbie?"

"Sure." He lumbered over to the elevator. When we were all inside, he used a key to access the floor marked "Gym."

The elevator doors opened directly into the cozy gym. No sign-in table. No security cameras. Lots of machines and a free weights area in the far corner.

"Very nice. I see what you mean by old style." Ideas for the tour flowed through my head as I moved toward the far wall full of tall windows that bowed out, overlooking the Pacific Ocean. "What a view! This would inspire me to stay on the treadmill a while."

I stepped forward but halted abruptly. We were not alone.

"I'm terribly sorry for interrupting you," I said to the woman on the rowing machine.

"Who are you talking to?" Maya stopped beside me and screamed.

I jumped like a kangaroo with fleas. Then I looked closer. Maya had seen what I'd missed. The woman wasn't resting. She was slumped over, and her hair wasn't red. Her skull had been torn open like a blood orange, and a lopsided, bloody circle stood out like a fresh brand on her plump cheek. Robbie seized my upper arm, but I couldn't voluntarily look away.

He dragged me to the elevator. "Leave now."

Marc grabbed Maya's hand as they joined me. He clenched his jaw, his eyes narrowed, but he said nothing until we all got out on the ground floor where Robbie called it in.

"What a horrible accident!" Maya's voice shook.

"That was no accident," I said.

"What do you mean?" Marc asked.

Robbie narrowed his eyes at me.

"Did you see the mark on her cheek? It looked like a bite to me."

"Who would do something like that?" Maya sobbed and buried her face in Marc's chest.

He held her tightly until she stopped crying. "She might have hit her cheek on the equipment. No one would do that. Except…"

"A maniac," I said.

"That's a private gym," Marc said. "So, it couldn't have been a stranger skulking on campus."

"Staff?"

He shook his head. "Unlikely. Robbie and the staff would be the first suspects because they're known to be here, and they won't have readily available alibis."

"Who else…?" But I knew. Anyone else staying in the building over the break would have access to the private gym.

"The members of the Black Triangle Club who're staying there and would have privileges," Marc said.

Chapter 3

I shivered. "We need to find out more about them."

"That's your first concern?" Marc asked.

Maya looked up. "You're not serious!"

"Leave. Now." Robbie waved his hands at us, and we moved toward the parking lot.

"This place will be swarming with cops soon. Particularly, if it wasn't an accident." Marc stroked Maya's hair. "They won't let us back on campus. I'm afraid your project has hit a wall."

That hadn't occurred to me. "Not if I have anything to say about it."

He loomed above me, looking a bit like a storm cloud on stilts. "You don't."

"Marc, I like you, but you don't know me. Not yet, anyway."

I surprised myself with that remark. I wasn't the kind of person who took charge, who rushed the line. I was the housewife who... No, I wasn't. Funny how our memories shape our identity. But my new life had given me the chance to change my narrative. I could tell a new story. Since my world flipped over, crashed, and burned after the divorce from Phil the Rat, I'd become a survivor. Come hell or a bad hair day, I wasn't going to let a paying job slip through my fingers. Uh-uh. No way.

Apparently, I wasn't inscrutable. From Marc's

reaction, I guessed that all my emotions had flashed across my face.

He stared at me, one eyebrow raised, and something approaching a wry smile twisted his mouth. "Why do I have a bad feeling about this?"

"Don't worry. I'll figure it out." I hesitated. "You are still willing to do this, aren't you?"

He glanced down at Maya and then back at me. He frowned, and his mouth worked, but he nodded. "I need the work."

My shoulders relaxed. "Thank you. I mean that. My finances are sketchy at best, too."

He grinned. "No explanation necessary. I'm an actor."

I laughed. "I'll get hold of Ricardo and Mia to fill them in."

Marc nodded. "I'm taking Maya home. You have my number. Keep me posted."

"You got it. Do you need a ride?" I gestured toward my olive-green sport utility vehicle.

"I have my bike."

I glanced over at a black motorcycle and wondered if Maya would have the strength to hang on to him after her shock. I needn't have worried. She got on behind him, leaned against his back, and wrapped her arms around his waist.

Before taking off, he reached down to touch her hands.

I smiled, then remembered the woman with the bun who'd tried to chase us off. I called Mia and filled her in on the murder and the delay, including the details about the Black Triangle.

As I finished the call, George Ho and Rusty

Riordan drove up in an unmarked car. Rusty appeared to have made detective. I waved. They glanced over at me and then talked between themselves for a few minutes before getting out of the car and approaching me.

George's handsome face was marred by his annoyed scowl. Rusty ignored me.

"Hi, George. At least the body isn't on my beach this time." I tried to sound cheerful and upbeat, although I breathed shallowly.

"But you found a body again, right?"

The storm moving in from the ocean matched his expression. As the skies darkened, a street light blazed on nearby, highlighting his short, dark hair.

"Sort of. We were all together with Robbie. He was showing us the old gym."

Robbie strode up next to me. "You need to leave the area."

"But I think they may need to talk to me." I gestured toward George.

He smiled faintly. "We know where you live." He made it sound ominous.

I silently sought help from all three in turn and met a wall of resistance. I sighed. "Okay, I'm going."

I'd try to wheedle a look at crime scene photos later. I had, after all, seen the real thing. I ambled toward my car while listening to the two detectives and the campus cop exchange information. Nothing that I didn't already know.

I drove home, my head full of questions, the main one being why? Who would even know about a woman exercising in a little-used facility during a holiday break? It would be an odd place for someone to randomly stumble upon her for an opportunistic—what?—robbery?

In any case, Mia, Ricardo, and I would have to regroup at my place to discuss our options for continuing to make the tour.

****

My little blue, navy, burgundy, and white cottage glowed from the lamp I'd put on a timer. The porch light shone as my presence triggered the motion sensor. As I entered my front door and hung my keys on the hook, Doris and Thor greeted me, talking at once. I held up a hand.

"Stop! I can't understand either one of you." Although why I thought I could understand my cat was beyond me.

Thor scowled and stalked off toward the kitchen. His message was clear: *feed me*.

Doris shimmered and shimmied as only a ghost can. "Thor won't cooperate! You have to feed the beast before you leave so that I can inhabit him and have some freedom. I'm bored, and I want to go exploring." She sat in mid-air, crossing her legs and arms.

"Jeez, everyone's crabby."

When she wanted to leave my bungalow and the surrounding property, Doris had to find a creature to inhabit or possess. She preferred to use Thor largely because he'd head home when he got hungry, and she didn't have to try to steer him. When the two were combined, I called them Thoris, a name from my childhood when I read books about Dejah Thoris, Princess of Mars.

I went into the kitchen to feed my huge black furball of a cat. "I was going to share what I found on

25

campus this morning, but I guess you wouldn't be interested in a dead body since you're so bored."

Doris materialized on the counter in front of me. I dropped the can of cat food, narrowly missing Thor and my own feet.

"Crap! Don't do that!"

"Body? You found another body? Why couldn't you find it on the beach where I could see it?"

I picked the can up and opened it. "I had nothing to do with where she died."

"A woman? It's a woman this time?"

"As far as I could tell." I dumped the food in the cat bowl and plumped it up with a fork.

"Deets. Give me deets."

"You know we're making a video." I set the bowl on the rubber mat on the floor.

I barely got my hand out of the way before Thor started chowing down.

Doris nodded, her bangle earrings swinging silently.

"We toured the campus, looking at various locations that would be interesting to prospective students, including the old gym." I thought about what I'd seen. "Did people use gyms in the Twenties when you were alive?" I wondered if it had been a gym back then.

"People have been using gyms for thousands of years."

That answer was a bit cagey for Doris.

"Did you ever go to a gym?"

A smile played across her red bow lips. "I'd go to watch, and sometimes I'd do some exercises."

I was surprised women were allowed in gyms.

"What did you wear? I'm having a bit of trouble seeing you in modern workout clothes." I should have bitten my tongue because she took it as a challenge.

Doris went through a series of quick changes from a yoga outfit to sweats to 1980s-style tights to tap dance shorts and then stopped with wide-legged pants with a nice crease down the front and a floral print blouse with darts that was tucked in. "This is what I wore most of the time. Sometimes I wore my beach pajamas."

"Beach pajamas?"

"Is there an echo in here?" She changed to long, flowing pants, a contrasting top, and a little, loose jacket in the same color and fabric as the pants.

"I like it."

She relaxed. "I did, too. I would have worn pants all the time if I could have. Daddy said it wasn't proper."

"You were ahead of your time."

She beamed at me. "So, the body was in a gym?"

"Oh, yeah. Almost forgot." I told her what happened. "You look positively ghoulish."

Her eyes were wide. "Did you mean to make a joke?"

"Why do you enjoy dead bodies?"

"Because I am one?"

I shivered. I needed something hot and caffeinated to warm me inside and out. I set about making hot chocolate. I never understood people who paid for packets of instant cocoa or pods. Why pay extra for bad-tasting "instant" cocoa when it's already instant food? Just cocoa powder, sugar, and milk. What could be easier?

"Doris, I'm going to sit." I sat down hard on a chair

at my trestle table.

"You're having a reaction."

"I know." Suddenly light-headed, I bowed my head and inhaled deeply three times as my rapid pulse returned to normal. I sucked in another few breaths just to be on the safe side before standing up again. I still felt a bit fuzzy.

The rhythmic rapping at the door told me Ricardo and Mia had arrived.

"C'mon in," I yelled.

They piled in the door and hung their coats on my old wooden hall tree.

Mia beat him into the kitchen. "Are you okay?"

"No," I said bluntly. "I replayed what I saw, and my stomach flipped over. The woman's skull was ripped open. Blood and gore splattered the area." I laid my hand on my stomach.

They sat down on either side of me.

Mia asked, "What can we do?"

I took a deep breath. "Sorry."

Mia patted my shoulder. Her eyebrows peaked, and she looked really worried.

"I'll be all right. It's not as if I haven't seen a dead body before." I smiled at her. "Marc took Maya home. He got some shots and some video before we found the body. We need to get together with them to figure out a way forward. The campus is shut off for now."

But only for humans. I scanned the counter, but Doris was no longer there. The cat bowl was empty. I wondered if they'd gone walkabout.

"Doris?"

No answer.

Ricardo raised his eyebrows.

"Humans can't go on campus, but we have a four-legged spy if she's around."

"We don't want her eating the evidence," Ricardo said.

"Eeww!" Mia made a face.

"Gross, Ricardo. Now I have to try to get that image out of my head."

Doris materialized. "In some parts of the world, brains are considered a delicacy."

"Zombies," Ricardo said.

"Not quite what I was thinking," Doris retorted.

I raised my hands. "I really need you guys to stop."

"Sorry." Mia elbowed Ricardo. "What can we do to help?"

"Doris, if Mia and Ricardo drive Thoris over to campus, can you manipulate Thor close to the gym and the police? Maybe eavesdrop? See what you can see?"

"Sure. I'll get a wiggle on. Remember that I'll be seeing and hearing as a cat. I can't leave his body once I possess him. We are bonded as Thoris and inseparable, as far as I know, until we return to the invisible bubble I'm imprisoned in here."

"Do you really feel imprisoned?" I liked having Doris as a roomie, and it saddened me that she felt like a prisoner.

"How would you feel if you couldn't leave your house and yard except by inhabiting other living creatures? Eating mice? Licking your—"

I held up a hand. "Okay. Got the picture."

Mia giggled.

Ricardo snorted. "And you thought zombies were bad."

I stood up. "Thanks for coming over. I'm feeling

better now. I'll call to see how Maya's doing. We can still plan the tour based on what we've done and the old version. We'll need the voiceover stuff and enhancements. Don't come back without my cat."

"Don't worry."

But I did until I called Marc and he invited me over to his place. Turned out Marc had taken Maya home with him to nurse her back to health, and Theda had joined them.

Marc's apartment was eclectic: lots of free decorations like plants, rocks, driftwood, and shells. Big canvas paintings, frameless with no glass, so I guessed they were oils. Realistic but not photorealistic. Comfortable furniture in harmonious nature colors with plenty of open space and small tables for the plants and found objects. He had a stash of vinyl records. Nice. He was neat and organized. No clutter. No dropped socks. But it felt lived in. Cozy. Suited his personality.

"Coffee?"

Maya and I said "yes" enthusiastically and simultaneously.

Theda giggled. "Make that three."

It only took him minutes to make our cappuccinos, dump some biscotti on a plate, and join us. "You'll need some voice actors to explain what viewers are seeing in addition to anyone who appears on screen. Different genders and ages and accents would be good."

"What about you?" I asked.

"Happy to. I've done a couple of audio books. Your neighbor Mina has also done some voice acting."

"Mina? Really?"

He nodded. "She's very good."

"Is everyone an actor?"

Theda laughed. "There's a cattle call for extras in San Francisco right now."

"Cattle call?"

"That's an open call, in this case for extras. You know all those scenes you see with people in them? Those aren't passersby; those are extras trained not to gawk at the actors, clap on cue, and laugh at jokes they hear for the thirteenth time."

"I hadn't thought about it. I guess I assumed they were ordinary people. I've certainly heard of extras."

"Do you ever stay for the credits?"

Embarrassed now, I shook my head.

"It takes a lot of people to make two hours of entertainment," Theda said.

Maya cut in. "We can find acting students and some faculty who'll do voiceovers. It all happens in post-production, anyway."

"True," Theda added. "There are enough of us locally to populate the areas we want people in. Hey, who doesn't want to be in a movie?"

"Of sorts." Maya laughed.

"It's a credit!"

I sipped my coffee, relishing the airy foam over the steamed milk and rich espresso. "I'm curious. What's Marc short for?"

"Does it have to be short for something?" He looked at me sideways.

"No, I guess not, but it usually is."

He sighed. "Marcus Aurelius MacKinnon. I'm from the Midwest originally. My father was a classics professor at a small college, and, no, you've never heard of it. When I left for college, I started going by

Marc."

Maya ruffled his hair. "He's much cuter than the emperor."

Marc looked at Maya through his mussed hair with one eye closed.

I hated to throw cold water on such a sweet moment, but I had to know. "What did you capture on film, Marc?"

He ran his fingers through his hair to get it out of his eyes. "Quite a lot actually." He looked around, located his computer, set it on the table, and brought up the stills he'd taken. Using two monitors, he loaded the original tour and his video side by side. "Maya, can you hand me the spreadsheet on the printer?" He took it from her, rearranged the sheets, and handed it to me. "Before we met you, I roughed out potential shots."

I followed along as he went through what he'd captured so far. "Did you stop shooting at the gym?"

"No, actually." He put a grid of still shots on one monitor and a rough video on the other.

Some of the shots were framed, but others showed floor, ceiling, or walls. Some were blurry, but all had audio.

"Stop!"

But Marc had already paused the feed. "This is what I wanted to show you."

He'd caught the body on both media. The pictures were shot from the hip but clear. The video was less helpful due to a lack of focus.

I leaned closer as he went slowly through the photos. "This is great. You captured more than I thought."

"I printed a few out." He laid them out on the table

and started putting them in order.

I took over sorting through the pictures, spreading them out as I did, establishing the sequence. I looked up and realized that Maya and Marc were watching me. I pulled back and let go of the photos. "I'm sorry. Go ahead." I clasped my hands.

Marc stared at me, his left hand holding the elbow of his right arm, right hand on his chin.

"No." He stared down at the picture scramble. "Look what you've done." He pointed.

I followed his gesture and saw the pattern. Marc's pictures had captured Robbie's body language. He clearly led us to the body. I remembered the conversation. For the tour, it wasn't a hot spot. We'd talked about the newer gym nearby that the students would use. We would have cut the shots of the old gym despite its lovely view.

We were there because of Robbie. Marc's camera caught him peeking back over his shoulder as if to make sure we were following, something I hadn't noticed at the time. He led us into the elevator, making him the last out and us the ones who saw the body first. I locked eyes with Marc.

"Did he want us to find it?"

"That's what it looks like to me."

I scanned the photos again. "Somehow, you got the bite mark in focus."

"I'm good." He grinned. "I had to work for that shot. Robbie was already herding us out."

I sorted out the pictures of the victim. "If this was an accident, it was a horrific one. A piece of her skull is missing." I scanned through the rest of the prints. They weren't as precise as crime scenes photos, and I couldn't be sure about blood splatter or what might have caused the wound. What had happened to this woman and why? Was Robbie involved?

Maya kept her distance from the photos. "The upside is you don't need to include the old gym. I think we could return to campus tomorrow if we keep to the other end."

I nodded. "Such a beautiful campus. Weather projections call for bright days this week. We'll have to put off the Student Union shots. We can pick classrooms further away. We'll have to be super sweet to everyone." I narrowed my eyes at Marc and Maya. "You two should make the requests."

Marc frowned. "Why?"

I winced. "I have history with some of the cops."

He raised an eyebrow. "Are we working with a criminal?"

Maya's laugh rescued me. "She has the hots for George."

"The cop?" His eyes widened.

Maya nodded and grinned.

"Hey!" I protested.

"It's true, though, isn't it?"

She had me there. "We're old college friends."

"Friends?" she said.

I sighed. "We used to date."

"*Used to*?"

"Maya!"

She chuckled again.

I looked up at Marc. "We're exploring a rekindle." I wasn't sure I liked the knowing smile on his face. "Moving on. Think we can get the shots in the next couple of days?"

"Sure. If we don't find any more bodies."

"Bite your tongue."

Chapter 4

I pulled up on my half-sandy, half-scraggly grass front yard, took a moment to smell the salty air, and headed into my little California bungalow. Immediately, a ghost and a very hungry cat attacked me. When he's inhabited by Doris, she runs him ragged.

Despite the icy fingers Doris poked through various parts of my body, I made it to the kitchen and dumped a can of cod-flavored cat food in Thor's bowl. I rounded on Doris.

"Stop!"

She froze, one finger outstretched, ready to jab me in the shoulder.

I took a deep breath. "Okay. What did you guys find out?"

"Wellllllllll." She stretched the word out maddeningly.

I wanted to smack her but knew that I'd be the one to suffer. Passing any body part through a ghost is a decidedly unpleasant experience. It's like a cross between touching moldy gelatin and rancid whipped cream. So I waited.

She preened as if she could actually straighten the black feather extending upward from her sequined headband.

"Did you really go on campus wearing a flapper outfit, knowing that the occasional person will be able to see you, if only peripherally?"

Doris pouted. "I wore this." In an instant she looked like a modern college student in jeans, boots, and a jacket. She kept her hair in its neat, dark bob, and her lips were a brighter red than the current fashion. "Now, do you want to know what we found out?"

"Without a doubt."

She made a *moue*. "George saw us." Her voice was hushed with excitement.

"Did he send you home?"

She shook her head. "He took us up in the elevator. The body was gone, but there was blood everywhere. That redhead is making moves on him again."

Great. Just what I needed to hear. "What did they say?" Then it struck me. "Wait a minute. Cats don't see red and can't tell the difference between green and red. If I recall, the carpet in that room is green."

"The afternoon sun flooded through those huge windows, limiting what I could see even further. I moved under equipment and into corners to see better. Big blobs of darker color stained the rug and lower walls."

"Sounds like she wasn't standing when she was killed. We saw her on the rowing machine."

Doris nodded. "George and Rusty argued about whether or not there was enough blood and how she got her injuries."

I was delighted to hear they'd been arguing. "Accident or murder?"

Doris' eyes narrowed, and she smiled wickedly. "Murder."

My cell rang, and I jumped a mile.

Doris giggled.

I shot her a dirty look as I answered. "Jack?"

"Hi, Sis. Are we still welcome for Christmas?"

"Absolutely!" My thoughts spun. I still hadn't done anything to prepare for their visit or Christmas.

"Are you sure? I hear hesitation."

I clenched my teeth. "It's only… I haven't gotten much done. You see…"

"No! Not another body on your beach?"

"No body on my beach."

"Good." His relief echoed through the ether.

"At the college."

"Pardon?"

"We found a body at the college. In the old gym."

Dead silence. I winced.

"Who's *we*?" His voice was harsh.

My voice cracked. "Marc, Maya, Robbie, and me. Robbie's a campus cop." As if that somehow made it official.

"I remember Maya from the Halloween party. Who's Marc? A new boyfriend? What happened to George?"

Baby brothers. *Grrr.*

"Marc is Maya's boyfriend, and they're helping me with the augmented reality tour. We were doing establishing shots. The body has nothing to do with me except to limit my access on campus when we're crunched for time."

Silence.

"Again with the long pause, Jack? This is my livelihood the murderer is messing with."

"Wait a minute. You said body. Now it's a murder?"

"I kind of sent Thoris over to campus to have a

look-see." I held the phone away from my ear as he yelled. When I couldn't hear him anymore, I said, "She overheard George and Rusty discussing it as a murder." I put the phone back against my ear.

"Have you talked to George?"

"Not really."

"As soon as Gillian gets home, we're heading over there. In the meantime, call George."

"You're going to hit rush hour traffic."

"We'll see you soon." He hung up.

"Rats."

Thor looked up.

"Not for you." I dialed George. "Hey."

"I wondered when I'd hear from you." The words would have sounded harsh without their warm tone.

"Are you going to make me ask?"

"You know how much I enjoy it."

"Jack's mad at me for finding a body. Must I watch the evening news to find out what's going on?"

"You mean your cat hasn't reported back yet?"

I swear I heard a muffled chuckle. "Thanks for letting him in, by the way."

"You should have been there to see me stall Robbie until I could round your cat back up and corral him on the elevator." There was an audible note of disgust in his voice.

It was my turn to laugh. "Doris was flirting with you."

He *humph*ed. "When's your brother coming for Christmas?"

"When he heard about the body, he said he was rounding up Gillian and heading over. I haven't heard back, so they could arrive tonight. They planned to come tomorrow morning. I need to stock up on a few things. I can always order pizza. Do you want to come over?"

"I can pick up dinner. If they don't come, you'll have leftovers."

"Suits me. How about that new Mexican place?"

"The Oaxacan one?"

"What's it called?"

"Variedades, I think?"

"I can go online to look at a menu, or you could surprise me."

"Heat level?"

"Try mostly mild with a few mediums. I never go with anything hotter on a first try with a new restaurant. Better bring some milk."

"Milk?"

"It quells the heat better than water or anything else. Just in case."

"Will do. See you soon."

I showered and then changed into black corduroy jeans and a black and white sweater. The house wasn't too bad, but I threw the paper in the recycling bin and passed the duster wand over everything. Still not quite there. I wet a sponge and rubbed it over the couch and upholstered chairs to remove the cat hair. Now I was ready.

Doris materialized in a flowing, pale blue maxi dress to announce, "He's here."

I paused to assess her choice. "Looking good." I proceeded to the front door to greet George. "Welcome."

He entered with a flat box and several bags and headed for the kitchen.

My cell rang. "Hi, Jack."

"We're close. Gillian's driving. Nerves of steel."

"Food's here. Just come on in when you get here. George came over."

"See you soon." He hung up.

I followed the delicious odors wafting in George's wake as he carried the food into the kitchen. "You should join us for Christmas. I assume you're not flying to see relatives in Hawaii, or am I wrong?"

George unloaded the bags. "I'm not."

As he opened the containers, spices mulled the air. "I'm salivating."

He selected a couple of plates from the cupboard. "For me or the food?"

"Guess which."

Annoyingly, he kissed the tip of my nose and turned back to the food.

I have no idea what got into me, but I grabbed him and kissed him. He initially resisted, but I held him tighter.

His lips softened under mine, and his head tilted down into the kiss. His right arm found its place around my waist, lifting me into him. I could have stayed there forever...

If the door hadn't banged open.

"We're here!" Something heavy landed on the floor.

George finished off the kiss with a flourish and let me go. We exchanged a longing gaze for the few seconds it took Jack to make his way to the refrigerator and grab a beer.

He tossed the twist top into the sink and took a long swallow. "Ah, I needed that!" Then he noticed us.

"Did I interrupt something? You're looking a little flushed, Sis."

Gillian strolled in. "Bad timing?"

"Not for dinner," George said gallantly, handing her a plate. "I picked up a little of everything, including a crisp with chili *verde*."

I elbowed Jack. "That's as close as you're coming to a pizza tonight."

He made a face at me but took a plate. "What sauce is this?"

George said, "Mole Amarillo. The restaurant is new, so I asked them for a selection. Consider this a taster meal."

"I could eat a horse." Jack loaded his plate.

George's face worked. Knowing him, he wanted to say something about horsemeat or some other creature being in the food. In the end, good manners won. I laughed at him silently behind Jack's back, and he smirked back.

Gillian kicked off her shoes and joined us at the trestle table. We ate quietly. The signal to talk was when Jack got up to get another beer.

"Anyone want something to drink?"

"Could you bring the pitcher of iced tea over to the table?" I asked.

"Sure thing." He set it next to me and resumed his seat.

I poured myself a glass and slid the pitcher across to Gillian.

Gillian wiped her mouth and neatly tucked her napkin under the edge of her plate. She lifted the pitcher and poured a glass. "So, George, we hear there's been a murder."

George raised his left eyebrow and turned to look at me. "Word gets out fast."

"You didn't expect me to keep it from them, did you?"

"Of course not. This one wasn't on Murder Beach. It was over at the college. I would appreciate it if you didn't go around calling it a murder just yet. We haven't released that information, and it is the holidays. We'd like to keep them merry and bright."

"Do you celebrate Christmas, George?" Gillian sipped her tea.

I was surprised, and a bit annoyed that she steered him away from the murder, but I reached over to the crisp and separated a large slice, careful not to dislodge the green chilis on the top.

"I'm not really much for American cultural Christmas. No tree in my apartment, but there are a few things I do. I grew up in Hawaii, so it was more about surfing and kalua pig. Hard to do on the cold northern coast of California. But my family wanted to be part of America, so we would meet for a big meal like everyone else. No one liked turkey. Very dry. No taste. So, instead, we had eight treasures duck, a whole duck." He made a circle out of his hands. "Stuffed with diced chicken, smoked ham, peeled shrimp, fresh chestnuts, bamboo shoots, dried scallops, and mushrooms stir-fried with *slightly* undercooked rice, soy sauce, ginger, spring onions, white sugar, and rice wine." He licked his lips.

In that moment, I realized that, although he ate pizza, he enjoyed seasoned, prepared food. When we'd dated as college students, we'd ingested a lot of fast food and mushroom pizza. I tucked that tidbit of info away to be used later.

"You're making it really hard for me to ask you about dead bodies after that description." I poured more oolong into my glass.

George finished the last of his drink and pushed his cup toward me. "Your name came up more than once in our interviews."

I refilled his glass. "Really? Let's see, Robbie would have talked about me and the film project."

George nodded.

"Have you interviewed Marc and Maya?"

George nodded. "Rusty did." He raised his eyebrow.

"Anyone else? A rather nasty piece of work with a bun?" I asked.

"She didn't like you, either. Said you were entitled. Felt you were suspicious, shouldn't have been there, and should be investigated for skulking."

Jack chuckled. "That's my sister, a major skulker."

I ignored him. "How did you run into her?"

"She sought us out when she saw all the cars and the building taped off. Told us right away about an upstart young woman and her friends who were up to no good on a closed campus. She felt you needed to be arrested."

"Great. Who is she?"

"Turns out she's a professor, staying in the Student Union to be closer for the reunion. I'm sure you saw her using the cane. But she lives in one of the condos the college owns and rents to professors until they can find their own accommodations. California rents being what they are, she never did find her own place. Her daughter is currently a student here, although she's spending a year abroad in France. Montpelier, I believe." He pulled his notebook out and flipped through his notes. "What did she say to you?"

"She told us we had no right to be there."

"What was she wearing?" He wrote my name at the top of a fresh page followed by Pascarini.

I frowned. "Are you interrogating me?"

"Of course." His smile was lopsided.

"Do I need a lawyer?"

"Do you?"

"Not yet."

"Good." He wrote something that looked a lot like *declined legal* upside down. "What was she wearing?"

"I'm not sure. She was short and dark, and her clothes were dark and nondescript."

"Did you see anything unusual about her clothing?"

"Like were there bloodstains?"

"Were there?" He looked up from his notebook.

"Not that I noticed."

"Anything you want to add?"

"Who the hell was she?"

"Oh, didn't I say? She's a professor—"

"Yeah, I got that bit. What's her name?"

George flipped back a page. "Professor Sophia Pascarini. History."

"Does she belong to the Black Triangle Club? You said she's here for a reunion."

"I believe I mentioned she lives on college property."

"You didn't answer my question."

He pocketed his notebook. "What's for dessert?"

"*George!*" I put as much whine in my voice as I

could.

He put an arm around me and kissed the top of my head. Probably guessed I'd bite if he got anywhere near my mouth.

"Who's the victim?" Gillian carried her plate to the dishwasher.

"That I can tell you given that it's probably already on the news. Mirabella Ramos. She was here for an event on campus and had used a guest pass to the building and gym. She's from Columbus, Ohio."

"That 'event' would be the reunion. Manner of death?" I asked icily.

George squeezed me and rose. "Ice cream?" He opened the freezer.

Jack said, "You know he loves teasing you, right?"

"Sadist!" I yelled. When I finished stashing away the leftovers, I wiped the table down.

George and Gillian served everyone ice cream. A bowl of coffee chip awaited me. I finished it before I asked the most important question. "Can we resume filming the tour tomorrow?"

George paused, smiling at me. Just as I felt like leaping across the table at him, he said, "Sure. You can't go in the building. That's still under our control. But you can film anywhere else on campus. We've already informed Robbie, so he's available to show you around."

"You mean keep an eye on us."

"That, too." George licked his spoon and set it in the bowl. "So, make your plans. Just don't try sneaking in." He narrowed his eyes at me, but the corner of his mouth twitched. "*We* will know."

Chapter 5

Saturday morning Jack, Gillian, and I drove over to campus in separate cars so that they could leave if things got too boring. Marc said he'd pick up Maya.

We all met by the white-domed observatory overlooking the ocean at the point of the peninsula. The sun shone down, casting glittering sequins on the waves, and warmed us in the chill of the salt air blowing in off the ocean. A few people strolled along the water's edge, walking dogs. Benches dotted the campus, and some were occupied, although it was too cold to sit comfortably for long.

The small observatory perched on a spit of land that curved out into the sea, providing a tiny, sheltered cove. That was our target this morning while the sun glinted off its dome.

"Doesn't it remind you of a sun-bleached skull?" I asked.

Jack's laugh turned into a cough.

Marc asked him, "Is she always like this?"

"Since we were kids. Back then, she'd say things like that to scare me. I'm the youngest of us two. While she was married, she went all funny and housewifely, but she's back now. How long have you known her?"

"A few days. She hired me and Maya to film the new tour, provide some AR expertise, and do some voiceovers. I'm an—"

Maya cut him off. "He's a wonderful actor, but we'd better catch this light."

"She's right." Marc set up, and they worked solidly for the next hour.

"Light's changing." Maya gazed skyward.

I said, "Why don't you get some shots moving along the paths through campus while the light through the trees is dappling everything. The campus isn't crowded. We can pose Jack and Gillian on a bench."

Maya used the still camera while Marc filmed as he moved along the paths. We passed a few occupied benches before finding one that was empty and in a picturesque location. I'd printed off permission slips for people to sign if we wanted to use their image in the tour.

"Jack. Gillian. Can you guys sit over there?" Marc pointed out a vacant bench that was framed by evergreen bushes. "Act casual but energetic. You want to be here at this school. It's *the* place to be."

After some fussing and adjusting, Marc got some useable footage until a clamor behind us broke the mood. But Marc stayed focused, turning smoothly, still filming.

Robbie ran past us and stopped near a bench we'd passed where a small, dark woman sat. I hadn't noticed her before. But now, she looked familiar.

"Cass, isn't that...?" Maya said.

"I think you're right."

"No doubt." Marc lowered the camera.

Jack asked, "What are you guys talking about?"

"The woman on the bench is the professor the cop was talking about last night."

"George."

"Yeah, him." Marc started toward the bench.

Maya said, "But she didn't chase us off today."

As a group, we moved toward the professor, and Marc raised the camera again.

"Stop!" a harsh voice yelled.

We turned to see George running toward us.

"Don't go any closer and quit filming." He loped swiftly past us. "I'll need that footage."

Marc fumbled with the camera. "Why?"

"Why not?" Jack asked.

"I think maybe we should leave now." I grabbed Marc's sleeve.

"Yeah." He nodded, and we all headed down a different path toward the parking lot.

"Cass!" George shouted.

Crap. "Why don't you all try to keep going." I turned toward George, who was rapidly approaching. "Hey, what's up?" I tried to sound nonchalant.

"Stop. All of you." George held up a hand. "You were filming." He pointed at Marc's camera.

"Guilty as charged, but you knew we would be here doing this," I said, still trying to keep my tone light.

"I'm not accusing you of anything. I want those cameras."

"Why?" Jack asked.

George narrowed his eyes and waggled his fingers in a *gimme* gesture.

"You can't do that! You know we need this footage for the tour. Let us at least download a copy," I pleaded.

"And I will return them to you as quickly as I can, but you may have caught something significant. They are now evidence."

"Evidence of what?" Jack asked. "Has a crime been committed?"

"George, what's going on?" I stopped Marc from giving George the cameras.

George raised an eyebrow, making eye contact with Marc.

Marc and Maya handed over the equipment.

"Thank you. Now you can leave."

"George!" I tried to look around him at the action going on.

But he turned around and strode to the bench, now obscured from our view by officers.

"Are they arresting her, or did she have a heart attack?" I asked.

"Serves her right."

"Jack!"

We returned to the cars and motorcycle. Jack and Gillian peeled off to their car.

"Meet you back at the house." Jack waved.

"I can't believe we got such great footage, and now we can't work with it. Without the cameras, we can't even come back for more." I felt like crying.

Marc and Maya exchanged a glance. Then Marc put me out of my misery.

"The cameras upload instantly to the cloud. We can access all the footage from today."

"As for cameras themselves," Maya said. "While they aren't cheap and we don't want them damaged or lost, we have more."

"Media majors start scavenging equipment with their first projects, and you learn quickly to improvise," Marc said. "Don't worry. We'll download from the cloud as soon as we get back to my apartment."

"You guys are life savers! Now the question is when we can get back on campus to resume. I'll call George this afternoon. He should have given us receipts, in any case. Maybe I can guilt him."

****

Back at the house, I met with frustration. Jack and Gillian hadn't returned. George wouldn't answer. I didn't want to leave more than four voicemails. Nothing from Marc. Even Doris wasn't around.

I jumped when my cell rang. It was Maya.

"Hi."

"Cass, you might want to come over to Marc's place. That is, if you're not busy."

"What's up?"

"We've downloaded the footage. Some of it's pretty interesting."

"On my way."

****

As I entered the second-floor apartment, I saw Maya seated at the table, looking at a monitor. "You were able to get the video."

Marc nodded. "And the stills. We didn't know what we were looking at initially. Funny how the camera picks up everything and is emotionally agnostic, whereas we only see what is important to us at the moment."

"What do you mean?"

"We didn't notice that she was dead."

"What?" I sat down hard on the arm of the couch behind me.

"Are you okay?" Marc asked.

"No." I stood. "Yes. I'll be all right. Let me see."

She'd paused on a very clear shot of Pascarini,

51

sitting upright, head bowed. The cop next to the professor pointed at her chest.

I squinted, not seeing anything. "What's he indicating? I don't see any blood." It would have been hard to tell on her dark jacket.

"We're not quite sure, but there's a spot of something here." Marc tapped the screen.

I saw what looked like a reflection a bit off-center on her chest. "How do you know she's dead?"

"She doesn't move, for starters. Her head is cocked at a weird angle. Also, after you drove off, Maya and I sat in the parking lot talking long enough to see other units pull up."

"Maybe she had a stroke?"

"They'd have been in a bigger hurry to get her to a hospital. We'd have seen an ambulance with sirens and EMTs rushing with a stretcher." He shook his head. "Nothing like that. No sense of urgency."

Good point.

"There's also this." Maya ran the video ahead and paused again, increasing zoom to show her cheek. "Looks like a bite mark to me."

"I think I understand why George isn't returning my calls."

That made two deaths on campus. But was it murder?

"Serial killer?" Marc asked. "Someone who likes fava beans and chianti? Are you sure you want to go ahead with this project?"

I weighed the options. Were we in danger if it was murder? What were the consequences if we didn't finish this job?

"Are you guys willing to continue?"

They exchanged a glance, and Maya nodded. "Sure. Financial situation is the same. We could use the money."

"And the résumé entry," Marc added.

I nodded. "That's me, too. It's the only job CaRiMia has right now. Ricardo, Mia, and I all need the money." I thought about bills and putting money aside for taxes. None of the local businesses we'd approached about websites wanted to talk about it during the holidays.

Marc gestured toward the computer. "Also, we have a good start here. Not only is there usable footage from the observatory, we have most of the campus walk we wanted. A lot to work with right here."

"I assume you want us to give you a copy of the raw footage." Maya handed me a flash drive. "This has everything so far. We'll be sculpting the final product."

"Sculpting?"

"Like sculpting, we'll cut away the bits that aren't part of the final piece of art."

"Thanks." I slipped the memory stick into my pants pocket. "I'll see if I can clear the way for more filming. I'm a little concerned that if a body appears every time we go on campus to film, they'll bar us permanently."

Marc pursed his lips. "I hadn't thought of that."

"I'm a little touchy on the subject, having been the target of a media frenzy shortly after I moved here. A body appeared on the beach in front of my bungalow." I thought back to that time. "Reporters showed up and camped out on my lawn as if the whole thing were my fault." My whole body shivered.

"I'm so sorry," Maya said.

I smiled. "No, I'm sorry for dumping on you. The

campus murders are bringing it all back. I have just to push ahead and get the job done."

Marc leaned back. "Agreed. Let us know if we can help. In the meantime, give us a call when you want us back on campus."

"Will do."

"One more thing, Cass," Marc said. "Did you notice that Robbie seemed to lead us to both bodies?"

Chapter 6

Back home, I stuck the flash drive into my computer and brought up the video, but now I was looking for what I hadn't seen as we strolled between the academic buildings. Thinking back, people were already walking through campus when we got there. Not many but a few. I saw nothing unusual until I got to the point when Professor Pascarini appeared on the bench. We were focused on getting to the observatory. I don't think any of us even looked in her direction, or we would have recognized her.

Scanning the video now, she appeared strangely stiff, eyes staring and dull. From this angle, I saw something that looked like a large, round brooch mid-chest. I replayed, pausing to look more closely. Her body appeared to slump away from the brooch. She wasn't propped up. *Rigor mortis*?

I continued to watch to the point when Robbie ran through the frame. I saw nothing that alerted him to the presence of a body. After he ran past, there was some muffled yelling. Minutes later, EMTs and officers arrived. Rusty and George appeared soon after. All of them walked through. Marc had not been focused on the bench at that point. As he realized something was going on, he pointed at the clump of people around the bench. Onscreen, I said, "I think maybe we should leave now." The video ended shortly thereafter.

Sitting deep in thought, thinking about what Marc said, I startled when my cell rang. George. My heart lurched, but I didn't want to appear overly anxious. I let it ring again before I answered, trying to exude calm through my voice.

"Hey."

"Are you all right?"

His tone of concern surprised me. "Why wouldn't I be?"

"I know you're aware that there's been a second murder."

"So, you're acknowledging the first as murder."

"It can hardly be avoided now with the body discovered in a public place. Too many witnesses..." The strain in his voice was unusual.

"George? What's going on? George?"

"Sorry. We need to talk but not now. Let Jack and Gillian know that a killer is on the loose, and they need to be careful, too. I'll get in touch with you tomorrow. You call me if you're worried about anything, understand?" I was touched by the concern in his voice.

"I do. George, I will call you if anything happens, but please take care of yourself. I'm assuming we can't come back to film right away?"

"Cass." A note of reprimand tinged his voice.

"Okay. Bad timing. You're welcome to come by any time. You know that, right?"

"Thanks. I do."

Jack and Gillian entered the front door, talking to each other.

"What's that?" The tension was back in his voice, making me wonder what he wasn't telling me about the murders.

"Jack and Gillian just walked in the door."

George exhaled.

"Good. Good. Stay in, okay?"

"We will. Don't worry!"

"Have to go." He disconnected.

"Who was that?" Jack plopped on the couch.

"George. He sounded stressed. He's worried and wants us to stay in and together tonight. I'm going to make sure the doors and windows are locked."

"I thought you installed a security system."

"Oh, yeah. I haven't used it since you left."

"Kinda defeats the purpose."

I sighed and armed it. The cat door squeaked, and I jerked.

"A bit jumpy?"

"I am. The strain in George's voice was palpable. Something weird is going on, and per usual, he's not telling me."

Thor stalked in and howled.

I looked down at him. "You are not helping."

"Cass, he's a cat. Just feed him."

I opened another can of cat food and set it on the floor.

"Are you guys hungry? We have leftover Mexican, cold cuts, tuna, or I can whip up some pasta and pesto?"

Gillian left the bathroom and joined me in the kitchen. "I vote for pasta. Do you have any sundried tomatoes or olives or maybe peas and onions we can throw in?"

Jack joined us. "Trying to make me eat veggies?"

"Always." Gillian fished around in the fridge. "Cass, why don't you sit down?"

"Yeah, we'll rustle up the grub." Gillian kissed him

on the cheek and then set a glass of lemonade and a napkin on the trestle table in front of me. "We went for a walk along the shore, and I get the feeling we missed a lot."

"Marc gave me a copy of the video he shot today. I should check the memory stick to see if the still pictures are there, too." I shuddered. "We walked right past her body on that bench."

"If there had been something unusual, we would have noticed." Gillian's tone was reassuring as she dumped the pasta into a pot on the stove and heated some of the leftovers.

"Would we? I'm not sure. There's something that's bothering me about her."

"Aside from the fact that she's dead?" Gillian laid the table.

"Well, there is that," I said. "It'll come to me eventually if it's important."

Gillian drained the pasta and mixed in sun-dried tomatoes and peas. "We should add capers and olives to your shopping list." She carried the food to the table.

I pulled one of the ubiquitous notepads over and started a shopping list, doodling an olive stuffed with garlic.

We ate silently at first.

"We need a cheerier topic of conversation," Gillian said. "Getting a live tree this year?"

"I'm so sorry! Yes, I meant to have it up before you got here." I helped myself to more pesto.

"I'm glad you waited for us. It's always more fun to do it together. Where've you got the decorations stashed?" Gillian asked.

"Under the eaves up in my loft. When you're

finished eating, can you get them down, Jack?"

"Sure."

Jack went up the circular stair to my bedroom, the only room on the second floor, which some would call an attic with its peaked ceiling. But I called it my aerie, and it was insulated and finished.

"Gillian, if we go out for a tree, is there any shopping you need to do?" I asked.

"No, we have everything, but I'll happily go along with you if you still need to pick up stuff."

"The only stuff I need to pick up is whatever will make us merry and bright!" I pushed aside George's warning that we should stay in and together.

Jack yelled, "Can I pass these down?"

"I'll go halfway up and pass them down to you," Gillian said.

We set up a bucket brigade for the half dozen boxes and stashed them behind the couch.

"We can get the tree…" I paused.

"What, Cass?" Gillian asked.

"George asked us to stay in."

Jack nodded. "The killer is really going to mess up Christmas."

"I can fix this." Gillian pulled out her phone. "Hello? Is this the Garden Center? Can I get a six-foot Christmas tree delivered?"

She winked at me, read her credit card number over the phone, and disconnected.

"We can obey George, get ready for Christmas, and spend some family time together." Gillian smiled and tucked her phone back into her pocket.

"You are really smart. Nice job marrying her, Jack."

Jack wrapped an arm around Gillian's waist and kissed her. "Nice job she said yes."

Within thirty minutes, we had our tree. Half an hour later, with a few skinned knuckles, Jack had it in the stand, and we were checking the light strings. Thor stalked through the mess we'd made on the floor and picked a fight with a stuffed Icelandic troll ornament. I started singing carols, and that reminded me of my recent purchase.

"You guys start with the decorations. I'll be right back."

With two bedrooms downstairs, I'd gotten in the habit of stashing stuff in the second one. I kept the first one ready for Jack and Gillian so that they'd feel they could stay over any time.

"Found these a couple of weeks ago and couldn't resist." I opened the box of glass icicles and the hangers.

"They're beautiful!" Gillian threaded a hanger through one and held it up. "Look how they catch the light!" She hung it on the tree.

"We can't do tinsel with an animal, and these glitter with the lights."

My cell rang.

"George again." I swiped. "Hi, George. Caught the killer yet?"

"Are you home?"

"Yeah. All three of us. Staying in and trimming the tree like you told us. Why?"

"Are the doors locked?"

"Yes, and the security system's on. What is it, George?" Even I could hear the edge in my voice.

"Turn it off, open the door, and let me in."

I did as he asked. "George, what are you doing here?"

"Cass, I can't say more, but this is a rough one. Please stay in tonight."

"Make you a deal. We all stay in tonight, but you let me resume filming on campus tomorrow. Deal?"

He sighed. "I can let you film on campus, but there will be officers stationed there. I will tell them that you'll be filming and that they should stay out of the shots."

"Please. This tour is supposed to entice students to come to the school, not scare them away. Can I hang up your coat?" I held out my hand.

"This is serious, Cass." He sounded tired. "I'm not staying long. I wanted to check on you."

"Can we have our cameras back?" I widened my eyes and tried to look innocent.

He shook his head and smiled. "You're incorrigible, but I guess they'd be essential for filming."

"Yes, they will be."

He hesitated. "All right, you can pick them up at the station in the morning."

"Will you be there?"

"Probably, but you never know." He had dark circles under his eyes.

"You're worried about another murder."

"Cass, we don't know if these are related."

"It would be odd if they weren't. Both women on campus."

He raised an eyebrow. "Not killed in a similar fashion."

"Are they both members of the Black Triangle Club? That would be the tie-in."

Jack and Gillian stopped decorating and watched us.

"How do you know about the Black Triangle Club?"

"I have connections."

"Ricardo," he guessed.

"Could be. I see you're not denying it."

He sighed. "We're looking into that angle."

I resisted saying, looking into that *triangle*. Instead, I prodded a bit further. "So, they *were* members and here for the reunion."

"How…? Never mind." He exhaled sharply.

I thought I'd push it a little harder even though he seemed exasperated with me. "Did the killer leave any clues?"

He narrowed his eyes at me. "You know I'm not going to answer that."

Jack went into the bedroom and brought out his computer, plugged it in, and opened it quietly.

"Okay, if you won't answer that, then you must have a limited pool of suspects given that it's winter break."

He leaned close to my face. "True, and guess who's on the suspect list."

"Not me!"

"You and all your little friends." George made a circular motion that included Jack and Gillian.

"Have you seen the height of some of my friends? Not so little." I retorted.

George snorted. "I'm serious. That's part of why I'm here. You all need to come down to the station and make official statements. You can have the cameras after you make yours in the morning."

"Ouch! That's just mean."

I remembered the first time I'd been asked to make a statement at that station. Not a very pleasant experience.

"I expect donuts and coffee."

He chuckled. At least I'd amused him, but he still sounded tired.

"I'll see what I can do. Remember, stay put and keep the alarm on."

"Will do." I let him out.

"Cass, come over here and give me the lowdown on the murders," Jack said.

Gillian rolled her eyes and hung the ornament she held. She put the lid on the box of decorations and joined us.

I sat down next to Jack. "Two women. Older. Alleged members of the Black Triangle Club on campus for a reunion this weekend. Secret society. Very exclusive. Mysterious initiation rites. First woman had her skull bashed in at the gym. Second woman was found sitting on a bench outside. I don't know how she died. They might both have had bite marks on their cheeks."

Jack kept typing into his spreadsheet until I ran out of things to say. He stopped when my last comment registered. "Bite marks?"

"That's what they looked like. You guys should come along to give statements tomorrow." I frowned.

"What is it?" Jack asked.

"Something Marc said about Robbie leading us to the bodies."

"He's a campus cop. Wasn't he there, letting you into buildings?"

"True. I'm going to call Marc and Maya and give them the good news about the cameras. I should also let Ricardo and Mia know what's going on and that we have some usable footage."

I made the calls, and Marc and Maya said they'd go by the station and then meet me on campus. "Jack, what're you doing?"

"A little research on the Black Triangle Club you mentioned. Not too much on the Internet. They aren't on social media. No website, at least not by that name. Or if they are, it's entirely private." He frowned.

"What?"

"One name does keep coming up: Hepzibah Cornelian. Strange name. Sounds like something out of the sixteenth century. Is that one of the victims?"

"No," I said. "I'd've remembered that name."

"The number three repeats, but that makes sense because a triangle has three sides, three angles, and three points."

"Nothing that would provide motivation for murder?" I asked.

He shook his head. "Sorry. No scandals or feuds that I could find."

"We have to allow time to go to the police station to give statements and get the cameras, but then we're meeting Marc and Maya on campus. They might have some thoughts."

Gillian returned to the tree. "Then you two lazy bums had better get over here and help me finish decorating. I'm not doing it all by myself."

"But, sweet pea, you do such a great job!"

Gillian lobbed a pine cone at him.

Chapter 7

I didn't see George when I entered the station the next morning, but the sergeant who showed me to a room to make my statement smiled as he indicated a donut on a napkin and a cup of coffee, along with the form and pen. He even shut the door gently behind him.

It only took me a few minutes to make my statement and polish off the donut, which was fresh and chocolate, my two favorite conditions for donuts. I thanked him as I took the cameras and left.

Gillian, Jack, and I parked in the lot near the dorms. The four buildings in the quadrangle surrounded a beautiful open area with benches and corner-to-corner sidewalks forming a large X in the center, as well as walkways along the side of each building. Marc and Maya weren't there yet, but George got up from a bench.

"Uh-oh. Is something wrong, George?"

He smiled and handed me a piece of paper. "No, in fact, it's good news for you. Given that the chief had a press conference a short while ago." He looked at his watch. "Should be over now. So, I can tell you that we believe the murder of Professor Sophia Pascarini is unrelated to the murder of Mirabella Ramos."

"No serial killer?" That was a relief.

He nodded.

"Less danger for us filming on campus."

He nodded again. "I'm still asking you to be careful. One of the killers might have seen you with cameras and tagged you as potentially dangerous witnesses."

"Gotcha," Jack said. "How do you know the murders are unrelated?"

I bit my tongue. I couldn't ask George about the bite marks because I wasn't sure that's what we saw on the professor's cheek, and it would give away that we had access to the video we shot and didn't tell him. Probably that wasn't technically wrong, but it felt dishonest to me.

"Professor Pascarini was killed with her walking stick. We think she was attacked while taking an early morning walk before the events of the reunion were scheduled to begin. Someone may have tried to rob or assault her, and she used the hidden sword in her walking stick to try to defend herself."

"Hidden sword?" Jack's eyes widened. "That's so cool!"

"Focus, dear," Gillian said.

I narrowed my eyes at George. "Do I have to ask?"

He laughed. "She was a linguist. She spent time in the Basque country studying the Basque language or *Euskera*. It's said the language is so difficult to learn even the devil gave up. While there, she had a *makhila* made for herself."

"A what?"

"It's a handmade Basque walking stick. Some have concealed swords. She was pinned to one of the old wooden benches by the sword, which has a very sharp, very narrow blade with a point that would slide into a human body easily. Her initials are engraved into the silver knob top."

"It sounds beautiful."

"It is. It's also illegal and may have been the object of theft."

"Maybe," I said. "But they left it behind."

"True. We recovered the walking stick shaft a few feet away as though when she unsheathed it, she tossed it aside. If they couldn't find that part, they might have abandoned the sword, or maybe they couldn't pull the sword free."

"Maybe."

"You're not convinced?"

I thought about it. "No. Don't mind me. I'm thrilled that you've solved it, and we can continue to film."

A very beautiful red-haired, blue-eyed athletic woman walked toward us.

I wasn't sure I liked the look on George's face as he watched her approach.

"Hello, Professor Byrne. I'd like to introduce you to Cass Peake, her brother Jack, and sister-in-law Gillian. This is Professor Libby Byrne. She's replacing Dr. Stone and teaching comparative literature and folklore."

"Glad to meet you," I said.

"Likewise."

Marc and Maya found us. They both had backpacks, and I guessed they had spare equipment with them. Marc smiled when he saw the cameras Jack and I carried.

George did introductions again. He repeated what he'd told us about Professor Pascarini's murder. "Which is why we tell people not to arm themselves unless they know how to use the weapon."

"At least she tried to defend herself," Libby said, smiling. "It bothers me when women just accept their fate without fighting back."

George frowned.

I looked around at the faces of all the women. George might not have liked Libby's answer, but all the women agreed with her. "George, you're outnumbered. Modern women save themselves or, at least, try to."

He nodded. "I understand the sentiment, and she did put up a fight. She had defensive wounds. But she was also old and frail. No match for her attacker, I'm afraid."

"Are you investigating that reunion?" I pointed at the banner over the door to one of the dorms. "The Black Triangle Club? What's that all about?"

George hesitated and narrowed his eyes at me.

I'd taken it a step too far. That was all we were going to get.

"I have to go. We'll still have a police presence on campus. They'll stay out of your way, Cass. Please let them know if you see anything suspicious." He smiled, but it didn't reach his eyes. "Or if you need them to move out of frame."

"Thanks, George," I said. "So, your investigation is centered on the campus then?"

"You have a problem with that?"

"No, makes sense. You know me. Curious." I tried to sound casual and uninterested.

He nodded, although I didn't for a half-second think he believed me, and walked toward the parking lot with Libby.

I frowned. "When did she arrive?"

The wind riffled Gillian's ash blonde hair as she watched them go. "They hired someone awfully quickly to replace Professor Stone."

Jack and I handed Marc the cameras we'd picked up at the station. He took them, checking to make sure they hadn't been damaged.

"She was probably a close contender for the position when they offered it to Stone, was still available, and wanted to accept."

"Mina is on campus, too," Maya said. "She was a member of the Black Triangle Club."

"Mina's a member of the club? She never mentioned it." Then again, there was no reason she should have. I really didn't know a lot about her.

Maya nodded. "She also said that, although she'd be happy to be one of our voice actors, her days in front of the camera are over."

"It's amazing that everyone's an actor of one stripe or another," I said.

Marc shrugged. "It's California."

I scanned the paper George had handed me. "Okay, let's go. We can film in this dorm, but we're not to film in that one with the banner. The reunion people are staying there and want their privacy."

Marc finished checking the cameras and set off toward the dorm a little behind us as he shot the beauty of the quad once we'd moved out of frame.

Inside, we followed behind him so that he could get clean footage of the halls and rooms. I noticed he took some interesting shots that weren't in the script, such as out the windows, lying on a bed, in bathrooms. I didn't question his artistic instincts. He had something in mind, and I let him work. Occasionally, he positioned Jack and Gillian and filmed them. At one point, he put me behind a desk. I tried very hard not to smirk or act self-conscious when he pointed the camera at me. How do actors do it? At one point, the camera was right in my face. I swear he did it to discomfit me.

When Marc was satisfied, we moved on to the Admin building, where Robbie met us and followed us around, opening and relocking doors. Our filming took on a more formal feeling. The offices were well-appointed with big desks and comfortable chairs and an air of scholarly opulence.

"Can we see a few of the professors' offices, too? I assume they hold office hours, so prospective students might be more interested in those offices as opposed to their parents who might be more concerned with administrators' offices."

He nodded. "I could show you a few in Heathlee Hall."

"Robbie, you weren't around when we filmed at the dorm, and everything was unlocked. Is that normal? Can anyone get in there? I notice you have to relock all the doors here."

"These offices contain private information and a lot of it. The section of the dorm you were in and the common areas are currently unoccupied. We could leave them open to better facilitate your crew. We'll lock them up tonight for the rest of the break."

"Is Professor Byrne staying in a dorm?"

"Yes, she'll be renting a condo from the college, and it'll be available for her to move in on the first of January. The college will give her a transitional week to get her things moved out before cleaning and reassigning her room. That's standard policy. She's staying in one of the suites, so she has a bigger space than just a single room."

I nodded. "Yeah, we filmed one this morning. Thanks."

We finished and walked out of the building. As he said he would, Robbie locked up behind us.

"Robbie, aside from the reunion people and Professor Byrne, is anyone else staying on campus?"

"There are some maintenance people and landscapers who work here during the day, but no one else stays overnight."

"Thanks." Robbie was here all the time. I wondered if there were other campus cops during the break or if he was the only one. "We'll be back tomorrow for more interiors, okay?"

He nodded to us and headed toward his office. He paused and turned. "Correction. There's Security personnel 24-7."

"Thank you."

He smiled and left.

Marc attached a lens cap to the camera. "Have you noticed that no one is talking about that first murder?"

"Uh-huh. I think they don't have any answers for that one. It occurred in a building that required key card entry. That really narrows the suspect pool."

"Is that why you asked who was staying on campus?" Marc grinned.

"Or the killer might have socially engineered his entry," Jack said.

"You mean, come in with the victim?" Marc asked. "With so few people staying here, that would be hard. Unless you picked someone up in a bar. Not saying it's impossible, but with this age group, that makes it a little unlikely. Not that I'm an ageist."

"A student or faculty member on break but with a key card? Back for a little vengeance? Or even earlier and messed with the door," Jack said. "Would Robbie have noticed?"

I held up a finger. "Or if none of those things is true, then there's a finite suspect pool, which makes me feel better."

Marc slung the camera over his shoulder. "Then we're swimming in the same pool with the killer."

Chapter 8

As we stood in the quad, a tall, slender, older woman in a flowing lavender dress and cape in a slightly darker shade approached us.

"And there she is," Marc said.

"Mina!" I greeted my neighbor. "I'm glad you're going to do some voiceovers for us."

"I told Marc my voice isn't what it used to be." Her voice was lilting and warm.

"You'll be perfect," he said.

When she smiled at him, the corners of her eyes crinkled.

"I was surprised to hear you were part of this mysterious club. You never mentioned it." I was increasingly curious about what I didn't know about her.

She looked down, and her smile was enigmatic. "My dear, there are a great many things we've never discussed. My membership isn't secret, but the club has become irrelevant in an age when people can search for anything they want on the Internet."

That puzzled me. "What do you mean?"

"We formed our little group out of a mutual interest in oddities, curiosities, and puzzles. We all loved to do research the old-fashioned way in libraries, museums, and archives. We loved factoids before trivia was a pursuit."

"That's what the club was about?" That was a surprise and a bit of a letdown. I expected something more occult, even sinister.

"Of course. What did you think it was about?" She tilted her head, reminding me of a quizzical bird.

I had no reason to doubt her, but I wasn't buying it. Her answer was exactly what people would say if they were hiding the true intent of their organization. "The dark arts?"

She chuckled. "You've been reading those children's books. Wizards and witches." She patted my hand. "Such a romantic."

Way to make me feel foolish. "But there are thirteen members."

She nodded. "There were, and that was by design. We might not have been the nefarious group rumor made us out to be, but when we were young students, we enjoyed the titillation of toying with the forbidden. We dressed in black when we met. I guess you would have called us the counter culture. We're called Boomers now, but that doesn't describe us. That's a socio-economic designation. We were searchers after truth. We organized in groups of three, so we were always seen as triads. We all had three names." She sighed. "I probably shouldn't have told you that, but I'm sure you already know that many groups have secret names among themselves."

So did witches. "What was yours?"

She shook her head. "That I cannot tell you. It's a secret known only to members." She waved her hands as if performing a spell.

"How does one become a member?"

Her eyes crinkled. "I'm afraid membership is

closed." Then her face saddened. "And we seem to be losing members to more than old age."

"I'm so sorry your friends have been killed." I reached out to touch her arm.

She nodded. "So am I, and so brutally. Who would want to kill a bunch of old folk?"

Who indeed? It struck me that she'd said, "there were." "I'm curious. How many members are here at the reunion?"

Mina's gaze dropped, and when she looked back up, her eyes held tears. "There were thirteen when the last of us graduated. We intended that our group would die out eventually, taking our secrets with us. An ephemeral secret society. The three you know about are myself, Mirabella, and Sophia. The other ten included Joe Pacenti, Tamsin Tredyffrin, Sentra Lee, Howard Castellano, Stephanie Bridges, Milo Coates, Jonathon Alcott, Sylvan Woodbright, Amanda Glen, and Mary Margaret O'Neill. However, Joe died while in the army, and Sylvan vanished in Nepal. Several years after her disappearance, her family held a wake, but I always wondered if she'd exchanged one life for another. She was born into privilege but was always on the lookout for the next adventure." Mina stared into the distance. "I prefer to think she's out there somewhere, riding a camel."

In my imagination, Mina, lavender gown flowing behind her, perched like a large blue heron with a tiny parasol atop a camel. I shook my head to clear the image.

"We're all older now," Mina said. "Perhaps soon there will be none, and that's as it should be."

A pall settled over the group until Marc said, "Not

you, Mina. You'll outlive us all."

She smiled affectionately at him. "I do go home to sleep at night even though I've been provided with a room here. I feel safer under my own lock and key."

I nodded. "Wise." So, there were nine left now. If they'd all come to the reunion, with Mina staying at her home, then seven of them were staying in the dorm and two in the Student Union. No, I corrected myself. One was staying in the Union, and the other was dead. "I'm looking forward to showing you the footage Marc's already shot. We've got a script, but you may have some ideas yourself, considering you were a student here. If you know any secrets, we'd love to add them."

I'd meant the comment in fun, but Mina thought a moment. "There are secrets here. Perhaps some of them could be given up now."

Marc perked up. "Hidden passages?"

Mina laughed, a high, fluting sound. "There are always steam tunnels and maintenance passages under and linking these buildings. Think of all the pipes and ducts needed to maintain a plant like this. Those must all be hidden away to maintain the pastoral image of a quaint college campus. You're only showing prospective students the glossy exterior. I don't think the administration would honor you for showing the literally steamy underbelly of the campus."

Her expression reminded me forcibly of my very strict seventh-grade teacher. I straightened my posture.

"That's a very good point." But I was still curious.

"But there was a book."

"A book?" I repeated.

Marc shifted and bumped into me, catching my attention. "Sorry, Cass. Heavy equipment."

"Yes, those cameras must be heavy," Mina said. "You'd better get going."

"But, Mina, I want to talk to you some more about the secrets of the campus and the book you mentioned."

"I understand." She waved and went back toward the dorm.

"What's the matter, Jack?"

"She gave us thirteen names, but she never mentioned Hepzibah Cornelian."

"Who?" Marc asked.

"When I searched online for info on the Black Triangle Club, one name came up a lot: Hepzibah Cornelian."

Marc smirked. "That sounds made up."

"I can ask her when I see her, but that might not be until after the reunion is over," I said.

"She may have forgotten by then," Jack said.

I shook my head. "Trust me. She is the sharpest knife in the drawer."

Marc asked, "What's next on the list?"

"We need some students to inhabit a few places to bring them to life."

"Ricardo and his gaming friends?" Jack said.

I nodded, pulled out my phone, and made the call. "We'll be shooting outside near the fountain, so dress warmly. Nothing outrageous. We want you to look like students that would appeal to a wide swathe of the population. I hesitate to say look like people you'd like to know because I know you."

Ricardo laughed. "Don't worry. This job's important to me, too. Tuition's coming up. See you in a few."

****

An eclectic bunch, representing various heights, weights, and ethnicities, straggled in over the next half hour. Ricardo introduced them as they arrived.

"You know Mia, and this is Lisa, also a tech wiz. Bai's in economics."

An Asian woman in a purple ski jacket that matched her hair tips raised a hand and nodded slightly.

"Tory and Thierry are twins."

Not that I couldn't have guessed by their height and red hair. Female and male, they were clearly fraternal twins, and their milk-white skin was startling. I kept thinking California sun and burns. Tory had impressive freckles.

"Danette, better known as Dani."

"Hi, Dani." She was a slender African-American brunette in a dark brown quilted vest over a red turtleneck sweater.

"Look what else I brought." Ricardo pulled a drone out of his backpack.

"You didn't!"

"I did. This'll be great. It has a built-in 360-degree camera. It has internal storage, but I added a microSD card. We can get thirty minutes of video at a time with an eight-mile range."

"I hesitate to ask how much it cost, but if it's useful and likely we'll use it again, we can reimburse you out of the fee."

"Cool."

Ricardo launched the drone and, after a bit of a rough start, got the hang of it. Maybe we'd get some useable footage.

We spent the rest of the afternoon creating and filming little scenarios around campus. Used to role-playing games, Ricardo's friends got into the spirit of the thing and ad-libbed like crazy, giving us loads of footage to choose from. With the drone overhead, we even had shots from different angles. Marc asked them to take off their coats for some of the shots to change things up a bit and suggest warmer weather.

Gillian played the role of a professor in one scene, chatting with the students and pointing at some buildings. Later, we'd add information about those buildings and some of the departments and courses of study.

Marc said, "The camera really loves her."

"I think my brother knows how lucky he is," I said.

After we were through, Marc suggested that we use the gamers to do voiceovers of the various scenes they were in. "You know that giving the viewers choices about which tracks to take on the tour means we need more footage than doing a straight front-to-back tour."

Ricardo pulled the SD card from the drone. "Here you go."

"Thanks, man. I'll return it when I download the shots. Maybe we can use it again to get some shots from the point of view of the ocean looking at the shore and the college beyond. Same thing for the planetarium." Marc frowned. "It would mean flying your drone over the water. Are you okay with that?"

Ricardo hesitated, stroking the drone. Then he nodded. "That's what we bought it for." He looked at me. "It's not mine personally."

"Practice with it before we do that, okay, Ricardo?"

"You got it."

I asked Marc, "Do you think we're close to having

enough footage?"

"I do. I'll check out the drone shots. With the additional footage I asked Ricardo about, that should about do it. I'll put together a rough cut for you, which will make it easier to see the holes. I'm not sure we really need views of professors' offices unless you were just curious. We can go through your checklist. We don't want to do the voiceovers and waste people's time until we have at least a penultimate cut."

"Sounds good to me."

He startled me by suddenly swinging the camera up and filming for several more minutes.

We all stopped and pivoted in the direction he was filming. All I saw was a man in dark clothes across campus, moving furtively in the shadows. He might have been half-hidden, but we weren't. We were clearly visible, with the late afternoon sun highlighting us against the darker grove of trees behind us. Whoever he was, he couldn't have missed seeing us.

"Was that Robbie?" I asked.

Marc lowered the camera slowly. "I don't think so. That wasn't the best angle. I was shooting into the setting sun, so he was mostly a silhouette, but we'll see what I can tease out. I've got a decent filter on this one."

Ricardo shook his head. "I don't think he was as heavy as Robbie."

"Should we call Robbie then?" Gillian asked.

Marc squinted in the direction he'd been filming. "Might not be a bad idea."

I called, and minutes later, Robbie marched toward us. It was immediately obvious to me that the silhouette was all wrong.

"Nope. Definitely not him," I said as Robbie joined us.

"Not who?" he asked.

Marc showed him the footage in the viewfinder. "We were speculating on who it might be. We've decided it's no one we recognize."

Robbie frowned at the image and nodded. "He doesn't look like he's engaging in any illegal activity, but we'll investigate." He headed off in the direction where the figure had disappeared.

"Maybe it's time for all of us to leave," Gillian said. "You know, just in case."

"Yeah, I was thinking the same thing."

****

Back home, Jack helped Gillian out of her coat and hung it up along with his jacket, and headed for his laptop. Flipping it open, he asked, "Do you remember the names she gave us?"

Gillian played with her phone for a moment and then set it down next to him. Mina's voice emanated from it.

Jack smiled up at her. "Clever girl."

"Aren't I just? I started recording randomly after the first body. Might as well use the tech we own." She patted his shoulder. "Type."

An hour later, Clem's Clam Shack delivered our pizza, and Jack closed his computer. "I don't know, Cass. This is weird."

"Oh, yeah?" I slid a slice onto a plate, grabbed a beer, and plunked them down next to him. "How so?"

"Hepzibah would make fourteen. Mina says there were thirteen members. Yet, Hepzibah is the most prominent. Her very weird name appears more than anyone else's in searches, but there's no day-to-day on her. It's as if she's the most visible and the most invisible of the entire group."

"Are any of them very visible?" I got the pitcher out of the fridge and poured lemonade for myself and Gillian.

"The ones with grandchildren. They're the easiest to track, and a few don't seem to have discovered privacy settings." Jack swung the laptop around to show me a page covered in kids.

Gillian sat next to him and sipped her lemonade. "You are obsessed with the Black Triangle." She paused the recording.

"Not obsessed. Just curious. Are they victims or killers? Her membership casts Mina in a different light."

Gillian bit off the tip of her slice and chewed thoughtfully. "Not really."

He took a swig. "Seriously? You always pictured her as belonging to a weird and witchy cult?"

Gillian nearly choked on her pizza. "Weird and witchy cult? Is that how you see them?"

He tilted his head. "Don't you?"

"No, not at all. Very normal." She dusted the crumbs off her hand.

He leaned back, mouth slack and eyes wide. "Seriously? Normal?"

She nodded. "Sure. Picture her when young. She would have been taller than average. In college, when? Mid-Seventies? Late Seventies? You have the dates there."

Jack opened the laptop again. "Yep. The club was in existence on campus for nearly the decade of the

Seventies. Not all members were in the same class, and some hung around for grad school."

She nodded. "Look at pop culture back then. Group fantasy games got their start in the mid-Seventies. Neo-paganism was finding its legs. Science fiction and fantasy underwent a resurgence. ESP. Mother Earth. *The Tao of Physics*. So, you're away at school for the first time, and California casts its spell. You can tell me from your research how many of the members were out of state."

"That would place them away from home for the first time and away from parental eyeballs." I joined them at the table with the lemonade. "But even then, most people didn't join cults."

"Didn't they? Depends entirely on how you define a cult. Pass the pitcher."

I thought for a moment. There were a lot of cults that made the news.

"The need to belong?"

She nodded. "Same reason for joining any group, but Mina doesn't strike me as the sorority type. She said they were doing research. On what, I wonder?"

Jack read from his transcription on the computer: "'We formed our little group out of a mutual interest in oddities, curiosities, and puzzles. We all loved to do research the old-fashioned way in libraries, museums, and archives. We loved factoids before trivia was a pursuit.' Her words."

Gillian sat up straight and stared into space. "Three names. I was thinking like a middle name, but what if Mina were Hepzibah Cornelian?"

That sent Jack on a mad dash to find all the Hepzibah Cornelian references on the Internet. He compiled them into a list and nodded. "Some of these fit. She was an actress even back then."

"Bad name for an actress." Gillian refreshed her lemonade.

"Maybe her third name is an acting pseudonym."

"Here's another thought," I said. "If all of them had fully-fledged other names with lives attached, who were they? And why lead two or maybe three full lives?"

Gillian nodded. "And why wouldn't someone notice?"

"Perhaps someone did, but we didn't have as much Big Brother stuff back then. No digital trails, for example. The Internet wasn't even out of diapers yet."

"But it was starting," Jack said. "You asked why they wouldn't notice. Maybe noticing was the point of a totally weird name like Hepzibah Cornelian."

"What do you mean, Jack?" I asked.

"I mean, it would be like waving a flag to get your attention," he said, typing a search. "If you did a search and the name came up, you'd know you needed to contact the other members, or maybe there was even a prearranged meeting place."

Gillian snapped her fingers. "Like a call to arms. Like blowing a horn to get people to assemble."

Jack nodded. "This year around Thanksgiving, an item about Hepzibah Cornelian attending a reunion appeared."

"That's a pretty exotic explanation," I said. "If they really had three names, I'd bet serious money that one of them was their secret club name."

Gillian wasn't giving up on her theory. "They enjoyed puzzles and mysteries. I think we should look more closely at the secret message idea. Codes. If my theory is correct, messages among members would become increasingly obvious as the Internet grew in importance. For instance, now, on some sites, you could post a notice of a meeting and have others indicate an interest. Earlier, you'd have had to post another item responding to the first to indicate interest. That was done in an earlier age with newspaper ads. Hmm. I wonder if online newspaper archives..." She leaned back in her chair and stared into space.

Doris popped in, scaring us all and breaking the tension. "George is at the front door."

Then we heard the knock.

I got up and let him in. "There's still some pizza if you're hungry."

He took off his jacket and hung it on my hall tree. "Thanks."

I handed him a plate, and he joined us. As he contemplated the two boxes of pizza, I asked, "So, what's up?"

He chuckled low. "I'm eating two slices before we talk. Most of my meals at your house get interrupted."

Gillian asked, "Rough day?"

"Beer?" he asked.

I got him one. "Must be off duty."

He nodded and leaned back, half closing his eyes. "It was an active day, particularly after you contacted Robbie."

"Did you find the guy?"

He shook his head. "Did you happen to film him?"

My cell pinged, and I looked at my texts. "I think so."

"Upload it to my email."

I texted Marc about George's request for the

footage of the dark stranger and sent him George's email address. "Done."

He wiped his mouth and stood up.

"Wait! What? This was a hit-and-run dinner?"

His eyes crinkled. "Thanks, I needed that—the laugh and the meal. Rough day. I will see you tomorrow."

He kissed the top of my head, grabbed his jacket, and slipped out the door.

"I feel used."

Gillian chuckled. "Don't be silly. Even I can see how much he cares about you. He was checking to make sure you were okay. You do realize you two do shorthand?"

I growled.

"Let's see what's on the news." Jack got out of the line of fire and collapsed on the couch with the remote.

Gillian went to the table where he'd been sitting and picked up her phone. "Hey, we didn't play the entire recording."

Jack paused the TV.

Mina's voice emanated from the phone. "But there was a book."

Chapter 9

We frowned at each other.

Gillian looked at me. "You have to ask her about that. It might be relevant if it's a diary."

Jack snorted. "Or a grimoire. *Bwahaha.*"

Gillian rolled her eyes and turned to me. "You didn't tell George about the names."

"We don't know enough yet. Besides, he didn't really give me a chance."

"Still, it could be a break in the case."

"I'll tell him today, but we should do more digging. It's only a theory now. Besides, he's probably interviewing the club members. He'll get that info if it's relevant."

"But Mina…"

"We'll see. We can't do anything more on the tour until we get the footage from Marc."

Jack unpaused the TV, drowning us out.

****

Marc and Theda showed up shortly after noon the next day. She appeared well-rested, but Marc looked tousled, and I suspected he'd been up most of the night.

"I sent a link to the recut footage to Ricardo and Mia. Give me access to your computer, and I'll download it," Marc said.

I opened my laptop and watched over his shoulder as he checked to make sure the download completed without any glitches.

He leaned back and said, "I can cast it up on your TV." He looked over at Jack, who had been watching a football game.

Jack hesitated. "Go ahead. They were losing, anyway."

Marc picked up the laptop, and we all joined Jack in the living room while Marc made the connection to my smart TV. I took the remote from Jack. As we went through the footage, I made notes with their suggestions on where to do voiceovers and where to add enhancements.

"Stop there. Cass, this is a major branching point. We have footage for four paths from here." Marc reached into his backpack. "Here's a copy of all the notes I took. I've listed all four and given the time on the video where each branch starts. You can run back to the starting point here and then fast forward to each one of these times to see each path individually." He handed me the notes. "When you write the script, you'll need to create the first part before any of the branches such that each branch script follows smoothly. Got it?"

I nodded. "I understand. If you don't mind, I'd like you to go through the final before we submit it to the college."

Marc zipped his backpack up. "No problem. All part of the service."

"This gives me a much better idea of what should be said where. We have a bunch of spots with branches, so I'll rework the script." I leaned back. "We need to get our talent for the voiceovers and dubbing lined up." I let the video play again.

"This really looks good," Gillian said as the scene

moved down the path to the planetarium.

Marc frowned. "I want to reshoot the bit near the planetarium with you, Theda. You're really stiff."

"I tried to tell you that I can't act." Her voice was plaintive.

Marc shook his head. "Being self-conscious is what's killing your ability to act. You have to 'go there,' to be in the moment, to be present in the character. Stop being *you*. You shouldn't work looking in a mirror or try to create facial expressions. You have to experience what the character is experiencing, and it will show in your face and movement. Walk in her shoes. Physicality will come as you move through the experience. You can't act; you need to be."

"You make it sound so easy." She shook her head.

"It is, and it isn't."

"And cryptic," Jack said.

Marc raised an eyebrow at him. "Ever try it?"

"In grade school. Couldn't get out of it. School play."

"And you hated it?"

"I like being me."

Marc turned back to Theda. "Want to give it another shot? I'll work with you."

She nodded. "Thanks." Then she gave me a furtive glance.

"Cass, let me know when you're ready for reshoots. I've also marked in the notes the times where I think scenes need to be redone. For example, the planetarium with Theda. She and I can work on that. Ricardo's the only other one in that shot. I'll contact him, and we can get it done."

He smiled at Theda.

"With a few rehearsals. Also, when you have final scripts, we can align actors with genders, roles, voice. Some people find certain vocal ranges more pleasing and want to hire only actors in those ranges. For this, you're going to want a wide variety because you can't know your audience. This will be watched by a huge range of people. Even though choices will mostly be made by incoming students, you also need to have their parents on board. The main narration voices should be reassuringly calm but not enough to put the students to sleep. For Ricardo's friends' scenes, we should use them unless there's an issue. Female voice when gender is mostly female and so forth. Sensitivity to diversity. I'd suggest a viewing party with Ricardo's friends. They're all young and pretty diverse. I think you'll get some good feedback."

"Gotcha. Thanks for all this. I really appreciate the suggestions."

My cell rang.

Marc said, "We'll leave. You should get that. Catch you later."

I waved them out.

"Hi, George."

"You need to stay away from campus today."

Of course, that made me want to run over there right away.

"Why?"

"There's been another death."

My breath caught. Gillian and Jack turned their attention to me.

"Who?" Don't let it be Mina. Don't let it be Mina.

"Jonathon Alcott. History professor at Tempe. Portly man, out of shape. No sign of foul play. Have to wait for the autopsy. But looks like a heart attack. They are all getting up in years."

I knew he meant the Black Triangle. "You don't think so, or you wouldn't be warning us off. You think it's another murder."

Jack and Gillian moved closer to me, and she whispered, "Another murder? Who?"

I held up my hand.

"He's been under a doctor's care. Ordinarily, we wouldn't be doing an autopsy given his health and recent medical care." George paused. "But with the other murders in proximity and his relationship to the victims, I have reason to doubt. And that's all I'm going to say about it...Please, Cass?"

I had plenty to do at home. "Okay, but we may have to shoot more tomorrow. I told Robbie we'd do the professors' offices today, and Marc and Theda have some stuff to reshoot, although they have to line up some others, so that probably won't happen today."

"I'll let campus security know that I'm the one who told you to stay home. Somehow, I don't think he'll be too upset. Let's touch base tonight."

"Works for me. You can do another hit and run dinner."

He laughed and disconnected.

Gillian said, "What's up? Who's been murdered?"

"Jonathon Alcott. George says he had a suspicious-looking heart attack. We'll be working from home today." I slipped my cell into my back pocket. "We have one less suspect." I called out, "Doris?"

Gillian frowned. "I've hardly seen her since we got here. I hope nothing's wrong."

Doris faded in, bedraggled. "Stupid cat!"

"I hope you're not referring to Thor."

I tried to sound indignant to smother my laugh at her appearance. For someone who could change what she looked like with a thought, it was rare to see her discombobulated.

"Huh! No, if he'd been willing to get up from his nap, I wouldn't have had to use the damn mouse." She lifted wet feathers out of her face.

"Mouse?" A bit of a chuckle escaped me.

"The only creature stirring in the house this morning." She went hands on hips.

"There was a mouse in my house?" I sat up straight.

"Don't get distracted. Yes, there's a nest in the crawl space. Call an exterminator. On second thought, don't. I might need them again. Anyhow, it took hours to get over to campus."

"I can imagine! Mice have such short, little legs."

"And then as we got to the body, the mouse started freaking out."

"Probably smelled death."

Doris shook herself and transformed her clothes into the beautiful seafoam green dress that I'd first seen her in. "Not that I could smell a thing, being dead and all."

"No, of course not. The mouse?"

"Oh, yeah. Have you seen that rotten ginger cat on campus? The big one missing half an ear? Well, the mouse didn't, so neither did I. Suddenly, I was being digested! Took everything I had to leave the mouse and enter the cat."

"The cat ate you?" I was truly startled.

"Yeah. Hell of an experience. But the cat was a bit

of a lamebrain. No cunning. Just instinct. Really hard to steer. 'Oh, look! A bird. Oh, look! A mouse. Oh, look…' Well, you get the idea. He munched his way here on a circuitous path. Ugh. You wouldn't believe what we ate. Even a snail." She shivered with disgust.

I was tempted to make a comment about *escargot* but thought better of it. "What were you doing on campus?"

"Aside from being revolted? I tried to find out what was going on. Saw Gorgeous George and followed him around. Lethal injection of potassium chloride, he thinks. Won't know for sure until the autopsy. Looked like a heart attack, but George ain't no dummy. He thinks the guy might have been poisoned. He's locked the campus down."

"Is Mina there?" I asked.

"Yes, and not happy. He said no one can leave, so looks like she can't go home tonight." Doris gazed at her nails, and they lengthened and developed a red coat of polish.

"I need to talk to her about the book she mentioned and Hepzibah. I wonder if George would let me bring some of her things to her? If she's spending the night in the dorm, she'll need toiletries and a change of clothes at the very least. I could bring her favorite tea, as well."

Jack asked, "Does this mean that the cops think the club members are the suspects?"

"They could be trying to keep them together for their own protection, but the murders did start after they arrived on campus," Gillian said.

"Yeah, but it was the club members being murdered! I need a beer." Jack went to the fridge.

"That doesn't mean it wasn't one of them," Gillian

called after him.

"Didn't Agatha Christie write a book about something like this?" I asked.

"Several. Probably the best known is *And Then There Were None*."

"That's it! We could take a look at the members staying on campus," I said.

"The murderer doesn't have to be staying on campus. Christie's novel took place on an island. The campus is on the edge of a town. Hardly the same thing."

She had a point.

"Water on only one side. I get it. But I have very few days to finish up the tour video. I need access to campus even if I have to solve a murder or two to get it." I was only half-joking.

Jack sat back down. "Didn't Ricardo have a drone? Maybe you could get some additional footage that way."

"Now there's a thought. I'll talk to Marc about it," I said. "I'm positive Ricardo will be on board. Nothing like a kid with a new toy. No matter how old the kid is."

"I think you should move ahead with writing the scripts for the tour footage in the meantime. Maybe we caught something on film that'll help." Gillian narrowed her eyes. "You might spot it while you work."

"Okay. After I check with George about taking stuff to Mina."

Gillian put her hands on her hips. "I'm getting the impression that this isn't about getting more footage. It's about sticking your nose in a murder investigation."

"No! Of course not. I want to help Mina. It's the neighborly thing to do."

She laughed as I called. I didn't even get a chance to speak.

George was swift and to the point. "No, you can't come on campus."

"And hello to you, too, George. How're you doing? Lovely weather we're having."

He sighed. "Hello, Cass."

"I was thinking."

He suppressed a laugh.

"I heard that. I'm trying to be helpful. It occurs to me that if you've locked down the campus, Mina might need some things. I have access to her house. If you don't mind, I could bring some things to her. I'd call her, but she doesn't have a cell phone."

He exhaled. "I'll ask her and call you back."

When he didn't say anything else or hang up, I said, "George?"

"It's nice of you to offer to help a friend, but I was trying to figure out your angle."

"Can't I be altruistic?"

"Possible, but not likely."

"George! You wound me."

He snorted. "Yeah, right. Okay, I'll get back to you." He hung up.

"He wasn't buying it, huh?" Gillian asked.

"It might still fly. Depends on Mina."

Ten minutes later, George called back. "Mina wants to talk to you."

I heard rustling. "Cass, dear?"

"I'm here. Can I bring some things to you?"

"That would be delightful. There is a bag in my

front hall closet and another in my bedroom closet. They already have the things I'll need. If you could bring those to me as well as the diary *beside my bed* and perhaps some of my oolong, that would be lovely."

"Don't you need me to pack up some things for you?"

"No, dear. It's all done. All you have to do is to bring those bags to me."

"Mina, I'd never expected you to have a go-bag."

"A what, dear?"

"Never mind. I'll bring everything. Will you meet me?"

"Oh, yes. I have a few things to tell you about taking care of my house while I'm away. I do have a number of plants that need watering."

"No problem."

"Excellent. I will see you when you arrive. Goodbye now."

"Bye."

"Mina has a go-bag?" Gillian asked.

"Two, apparently." I laughed. "Can you believe it? They're packed and ready to go. See you later."

I grabbed my keys and headed for the car.

At Mina's, the bags were easy to find, but the diary by her bed was well-worn. I opened it and realized it was from decades ago. Is this really what she wanted? I looked around and under the bed but didn't find another. I could always come back if it were the wrong one. That would be another great excuse to get back on campus.

Mina was waiting for me with George in the parking lot next to the quad dorms. I set the suitcases down on the sidewalk and handed her the diary. She looked at the bags and then up at George, a helpless expression on her face.

"Would you mind?"

If it had been me, he'd have declined with a snarky comment. An emotional war waged a battle on his face. His upbringing won.

"Yes, ma'am." He picked up the bags and moved quickly toward the dorm, stopped, looked back over his shoulder, and said, "Coming?"

She demurred. "Give me a moment to say goodbye to Cass."

"If I'd asked…"

"We only have a few minutes, dear." She handed the diary back to me. "Slip that in your bag. It's from when I was a student here. There's quite a bit that may be helpful to you."

George was back on the sidewalk.

"That was fast. He's coming."

She shoved my hand, and I dropped the book into my bag.

"I didn't want to alert him to the importance of the diary. I reread it to refresh my memory before the reunion. They will, of course, search my house as I'm now a suspect. I'm relying on you to solve these murders and prove my innocence and that of my fellow club members. We did not do this." She patted my hand.

There was no more time to ask her questions.

She turned to George with a lovely, almost flirtatious smile. "Thank you so very much."

"You're welcome. They'll be serving supper soon. You should come with me." He took her arm and cast me a suspicious look before walking off.

I drove home, itching to get a look at her diary. Apparently, I didn't do a good job hiding my emotion when I entered because Jack, Gillian, and Doris surrounded me.

"What happened?" Jack asked.

"Is Mina all right?" Gillian asked.

"You're glowing!" Doris said.

Gillian peered more closely at me. "You *are* giving off a lot of energy."

I pulled Mina's diary out of my bag and held it up. "A diary, Jack, not a grimoire."

"Didn't you give it to her?" Gillian asked.

"Of course, Gillian, but as soon as she got rid of George for a few minutes, she gave it back to me. She didn't want the police to find it in her house, so she used me to get it out. She said it would help us."

"To do what?" Jack asked.

I caught my breath. "To solve the murders and clear her name and those of the other club members."

"Seriously?"

I nodded. "Yup. You guys can quit staring now. What do you think?" I was breathless with excitement.

"You're nuts. What's for dinner?" Jack said.

"Your brother's a minimalist. Of course, we have to help Mina," Gillian said. "Does George really think her capable of murder?"

"I gather he does. The campus lockdown means that anyone on campus is suspect. I think that's a false assumption. The campus has been pretty much open the entire winter break. Maybe people couldn't get into all the buildings, as we found out while filming, but we've all followed someone into a building. It's not hard. In fact, people will usually hold the door open for you."

"There was that shadowy guy we saw on campus," Gillian said.

"Perfect example."

Jack said, "Feed me, and I'll help. I already have the starts on the spreadsheet."

I glanced at the clock and headed for the kitchen. "Give me forty-five minutes, Jack."

With Gillian's help, I threw together some sautéed scallops and roasted veggies, and we reconvened around the trestle table for an informal dinner.

Then I noticed Gillian staring at her husband. "I know my brother is cute and all, but you're married to him. You see him all the time. Why are you watching him?"

She pointed. "He's eating vegetables. Lots of vegetables."

Jack helped himself to more. "They're good. If you made them like this, I'd eat 'em."

Gillian shook her head. "I'll need that recipe, Cass."

"Not really a recipe. I cut up whatever veggies I have around. Sprinkle them with rosemary, thyme, and little black pepper. No salt. Veggies are naturally sweet, and adding salt kills that sweetness. Salt is the most boring spice. If you want salt, eat chips. Drizzle some olive oil. Roast on a cookie sheet at 350 for 20 minutes. Stir them a bit and roast another 20 minutes. Simple as pie."

"Pie is anything but simple. No salt? Really?" she said.

"When I roast a single veggie, I might add salt, depending on the veggie. But when I do a mix like this with some sweet veggies, I like the taste better with only rosemary, thyme, and pepper. I had a bag of baby carrots that are sweet, and I cut up the last of the sweet onions into big rings. With that much sweetness, I prefer the mix unsalted. If the veggies are not particularly sweet, you could even play with some other, more savory spices. You change the outcome by using different spices. Play around."

"Huh. I'll give it a try."

Jack kissed her and went for his laptop.

He sat back down and opened the spreadsheet. "Let's see what we've got."

I cleared the table and put the leftovers away. "Cup of tea or coffee, anyone?"

"Do you still have some of that lavender bergamot tea?" Gillian wiped the table down as Jack lifted his laptop.

"I do. That sounds good. I'll make a pot."

A few minutes later, I set the pot and cups on the table. "Let it steep a bit longer. I used loose, so pour through this." I set a small strainer in its holder next to the pot. "The strainer will rest across the cup, allowing you two hands for my lovely porcelain pot."

Jack leaned forward. "Is that a warning not to drop it?"

"Yup." I reached for the diary I'd set on the shelf behind me. "Let's see what we can find out."

Chapter 10

Gillian gazed over my shoulder. "What lovely handwriting! It looks like a spider's web."

"That's copperplate." Doris materialized on the kitchen counter.

I jumped and put a hand over my heart. "Doris!"

"What?" she said. "You're boring when you eat. I had better things to do than watch you."

"Sorry, Doris. What did you mean by copperplate?"

"It's a style of writing we had to learn in school when I was a kid."

"It's beautiful." I flipped to the back of the diary. "I wonder if Mina is into calligraphy. Looks like this diary covers one year." I flipped back to the front. "And judging by the illustrations, it's all about the club."

"She's quite the artist. May I?"

I handed the diary to Gillian.

"Mind if I take photos of the pages with these line drawings? Jack can upload them to the computer. I think a lot of them are relevant."

My first reaction was that the diary was private, but then again, Mina wanted us to read it and use it to prove her innocence.

"We need to see all the possibilities in this diary if we're going to help Mina. I'm sure there are secrets hidden in here, given that the club was all about information processing. Do it." I stood. "While you guys are doing that, I'm going to make the dough for the cookies so that we can bake in the morning. I'm thinking sugar cookies and gingerbread for traditional decorating but also some bar cookies. Maybe gumdrop or turtle bars."

"Sounds great." Jack didn't look up from the laptop.

"Are you sure that isn't too much? There are only the three of us."

"Didn't you once call my house Grand Central? With the number of people who've contributed to this video tour project, I figure I'll need refreshments in case any of them drop by. Plus, I'm thinking I'll give some friends a dozen apiece as presents."

"I understand. I withdraw my objection. Jack and I love taking leftovers home."

"If no one shows, more for me. Do you need help?" Jack asked.

"Not tonight. I'll work you to death tomorrow. Ooo, bad choice of words."

Gillian laughed and went to work on copying the illustrations. "I'll upload these, and you can expend your energy compiling them," she said to Jack.

An hour later, she'd finished. "Mina should illustrate fairy tales. I love these drawings."

I had a sudden thought. "Do you think she did the line drawings in her two ghost story books?"

"I'll dig out the books and compare them when I finish this." Gillian leaned over Jack's shoulder as he finished creating a document that contained all the illustrations.

He selected my color printer and sent the file.

Leaning back, he said, "Sorry about using all your paper and ink, but I'm printing two copies so we can all look at them at once. Her use of color on some of these might also be coded. One thing I noticed was all the symbolism. Without ready access to Mina, you may have to do some research."

Gillian straightened up. "Is the diary self-referential?"

"Huh?" Jack said.

"Does it refer back to itself? In other words, maybe the symbols are defined in the diary."

"Good question." I picked up the diary. "I think I'll do a little light reading tonight." I yawned. "I'll let you kids lock up. Dough is chilling in the fridge. Don't mess with it if you want Christmas cookies."

I climbed the circular staircase to my loft where, sometime in the wee hours, I fell asleep, reading Mina's diary. I dreamed strange dreams about fairy tales and mythological characters.

In the morning, I was no nearer a solution to the murders than I had been when I went to bed. I gathered my clothes and went downstairs to shower. Jack and Gillian usually slept in when they visited me. But this morning Gillian was sipping coffee and looking through the printouts of the illustrations and pages that were spread out on the trestle table in front of her.

I made cocoa. "Any revelations?"

"A few, actually. I want to look at the whole diary, but in copying the illustrations, we also copied quite a bit of the text."

"Really?" I put my spoon in the sink and sat down opposite her.

"See this?" She turned a sheet of paper around to

face me and pointed to a drawing of a group of fantasy characters. "There are 13."

"Okay. Magic number." I sipped gingerly. Still too hot.

"There are 13 members of the club."

I nodded. "You think each member is represented by a fantasy persona."

"I do. I think the writing may only be what she could safely say in words that someone else might read. Someone trying to read her diary for its secrets would probably skip the drawings, regarding them as doodles. I want to confirm that by reading more of the text. What I've read is pretty innocuous, although there are some intriguing bits. I think the drawings are far more specific than the diary entries about the activities of the club that were secret. I'm trying to associate each club member with its avatar. Then we should be able to tell who did what to whom." She passed me a sheet she'd been drawing on. "In case any current club member is holding a grudge for past behavior."

I read Gillian's suggestions for the drawings. "Dragon, unicorn, troll. That's harsh. Elf, djinn, leprechaun. I wonder if the other members were aware of their avatars. What is this one?"

"My best guess is a ghost or a wraith, and I think that's how Mina saw herself. She was the observer. Reserved and in the background. But keep in mind that these are only my guesses at what these drawings represent. I didn't find a key last night. Did you read anything that might provide more specificity? Did you find out more about Hepzibah?"

"No character key. I was more focused on reading the text and looking at or trying to interpret the illustrations. But yes to mentions of Hepzibah, actually. She's all over the place. I wonder if she's a group entity." I looked back down at Gillian's crib sheet. "Nymph or dryad. Centaur, satyr. Is this giant rabbit a pooka?"

"Yeah. I wasn't exactly sure at first, but the only giant rabbit I know of is from the movie. He's a pooka, and Mina is likely to have seen the movie." She pointed to what was undeniably a giant rabbit in Mina's illustrations. Gillian's drawing in her notes more closely resembled a large Easter bunny. She'd doodled a bow tie on it.

"Looks like an Easter Bunny to me."

Gillian raised an eyebrow at me. "I'm not an artist, so please disregard the interpretation in *my* notes. The Easter Bunny doesn't fit in with the other characters nearly as well as a pooka would."

"I don't know. Easter Bunny. Leprechaun. St. Patty's. No?" I coughed. "I think Mina has provided us with a code we can use when we talk about the club members out in public. But…a kangaroo? That's not a mythological character."

"I'm still working on that one. There are a lot of mythologies around the world. Maybe it's a magical kangaroo. If you didn't know about pookas, you'd be asking why a rabbit."

"True. Have you figured out most of their alter egos?"

"I can't be sure. As I said, I think Mina's the ghost. I think Joe Pacenti was the centaur. Died while in the military years ago. Stephanie Bridges for the mermaid. She was on the swim team here. Howard Castellano is a really tall, big guy. I'm guessing pooka. If those are all correct, that leaves Milo Coates as the leprechaun. The flaw in the plan is that there must be female and male versions of each of these creatures, even though I clearly think of leprechauns as male. It's a SWAG that I'm thinking in terms of gender."

"SWAG?"

"Sorry, it's a work term. Silly wild ass guess."

"Ah. Technical term. No, it's a good guess. We don't have a lot to go on." I sighed and sipped my cocoa. "I think Mina's opinion of my abilities is a bit high."

"You know who could help with this?"

"Who?"

"Ricardo and Mia."

I shook my head. "It's the holidays. Ricardo's Catholic. I don't want to intrude."

"Call him and ask. He can always say no." She rose. "I'm going in search of my husband. Seems he turns into a sloth on vacay."

I got up to put my cup in the sink and check the time. It was late enough, even on a vacation day. I called Ricardo and explained the diary and what we were doing. I hung up as Jack and Gillian emerged from the bedroom.

"Ricardo says they'll be over after they finish breakfast and run some errands. He's interested in looking at the diary. Gillian, there's a copy feature on my printer. What do you think? Should we make copies of the most relevant material?"

"You've got a feeling?" she said.

"Not quite sure, but I'm feeling a bit anxious. I don't want to lose this information. Jack's document and your notes are only part of the story."

"Better idea," Jack said. "We can scan the entire diary into a digital document. Just in case the original gets confiscated."

I nodded. We were on the same wavelength.

"Mina was worried about it being taken with a search warrant for her house."

"I agree." Gillian walked over to the table and flipped pages to a scrap of paper she'd stuck in the diary as a bookmark. "There's a very interesting alphabet in here. You know how they're usually A is for Apple and B is for Ball? This one is a bit different: A is for Antithetical, B is for Blasphemy, and C is for Cauterize."

"A bit gruesome and rather unlike the Mina I've come to know." I wrinkled my nose.

"No kidding. This alphabet listing doesn't just contain nouns as in a regular one, but it has nouns and verbs illustrated with the mythical figures we've been trying to decipher," Gillian said.

Jack made himself a cup of coffee. "It might be telling us about the people. Y'know their characteristics."

I looked down at the letters. "Hmm. B is for Blasphemy incorporates the leprechaun. Maybe Milo swears."

"Could be." Gillian frowned. "It looks as though she was creating a syllabary for some sort of code, but she never completed it. Interesting."

"My wife, the scholar." He took the orange juice out of the fridge.

"No. Sometimes people create codes when they feel they need to hide information. She didn't finish, so it begs the question what did she want to hide and why did she abandon the attempt?" I said. "I think we're going to have to marry research we do on the remaining members of the club with whatever we can glean from this diary."

Jack chuckled. "Time to invite George over for pizza."

Gillian got up for more coffee. "You also have the tour to work on."

"And it's three days until Christmas." My stomach clenched. Too much to do and too little time.

My cell rang. "Speak of the devil." I swiped. "Hi, George, what's up?"

"Mina needs something else. Do you mind?"

"Of course not. What does she need?"

"She says there's a pink plastic jar on the third shelf in her bathroom. It's labeled PS in her handwriting. Apparently, someone has a skin condition, and Mina makes her own herbal cream that soothes the itching. That's a quote. I'll come by for it because the lab guys will have to test it first to make sure Mina isn't going to poison someone."

"George! Mina wouldn't poison anyone."

"It's procedure to test any unknown, particularly homeopathic, substance that's being introduced into an environment where a crime has been committed. You must see that's common sense."

I wanted to accuse him of making that up, but I said, "Sure, I'll get it this morning. Am I dropping it off, or are you picking it up?" I had no idea if it was really procedure, but it did make some sense.

"Thanks. I'll pick it up. I'll call when I'm on my way." He disconnected.

I looked at my phone. "I still have to teach him

how to say goodbye." I tucked my cell in my back jeans pocket. "I'm going to run over to Mina's to find a jar she wants."

"Okay, I'll keep working," Gillian said.

Jack put his coffee mug in the sink. "I'm going out to check on my antique car, the one in the shed."

"Have you stashed another one somewhere?" Jack teased me so much that I loved getting the occasional dig in.

He totally ignored me. "Just in case George wants a look while he's here."

Gillian shook her head. "Boys. Toys."

Jack kissed her on the top of her head, snagged his jacket off the hall tree, and went out the front door.

I tugged on my coat. "Back in a mo'." I closed the door behind me and took a moment to breathe in the crisp air and smell the salt on the breeze. "What a gorgeous day!"

Mina's house sat up the hill with a spectacular view of Las Lunas Bay. When I reached her front porch, I looked out at the sunlight making diamonds in the waves. I felt at peace and was surprised at how much this place felt like home. After all, it hadn't been long since I'd moved here from Pleasanton after my divorce. I sighed and pushed through her front door, pausing to sniff the lavender-scented air.

I assumed she meant the bathroom on the first floor. As she'd gotten older, she'd consolidated her daily living down here. However, there was no pink jar in this bathroom, so it must be on the second floor of the old Victorian. I'd never been up there. I hesitated at the bottom of the flight but then made my way up, keeping my steps on the colorful Persian runner held down by brass stair rods on each tread. As I rounded to the second set of steps, I paused on the landing and looked out the circular window. The pale pink glass didn't hide the view of the bay and my cottage near the beach that was a squat mushroom compared to this grand old painted lady.

At the top of the flight, I started opening doors that I assumed had been closed to cut down on the heating bill. The first room was for guests and was quaint without being fussy. It looked as though it had never been used. The second door opened onto what my grandmother used to call a box room. I would have referred to it as a storage unit. It was full of ancient steamer trunks and boxes. An adjustable dressmaker's mannequin overlooked the room from her spot next to a very dusty window. I was betting it was the only dirty window in the house. I shut that door before any moths escaped.

Across the hall, the door opened onto a sunlit master bedroom with a four-poster bed in white, pink, and rose. At the angle the sun hit the bay, the reflection dappled the ceiling, giving it the illusion of motion. I nodded. This was her room…when she was upstairs. I wondered if she ever comes up to spend the night here. This room—Mina's aerie—reminded me of my own up in the loft at the top of my cottage. I smiled and shut the door.

The next door was the bathroom with three open shelves hanging on the wall. The pink jar was at eye level. I took it, turned to leave, then stopped cold. On the wall to the left of the door hung a framed pen and ink drawing resembling the drawings in Mina's diary. I took it off the wall and flipped it over to examine the back. Mina had signed the back with the date and the word "Hepzibah" in quotes. I frowned and turned it back over to examine it more carefully. It was primarily black and white, but there were dashes of color here and there.

I needed a magnifying glass. But I was pretty sure that all thirteen of the characters from the diary had been worked into the design of the long, flowing gown worn by a tall, stately woman of regal bearing with a wicked twinkle in her eye. I pulled out my cell phone and snapped pictures of the front and back and then carried both the jar and the drawing back to my place. I'd return the drawing before Mina came back, but I wanted to show the others the original.

Timing is everything. George's dark sedan pulled up as I reached my yard.

"Hey, there!" I waved.

He smiled as he closed his car door. "Got the jar?"

"Right here." I held it up.

"Great. I'm in a bit of a hurry." He held out his hand.

I hesitated, feeling a bit rebuffed. Handing him the jar, my fingers lingered on his. "Has there been another murder?"

Now he hesitated.

Aha. The little hairs on my neck stood at attention.

"Not a successful one." He took the jar, pulling away. "I have to go, Cass."

George looked me straight in the eyes as if trying to convince me of the truth of his words. He either didn't see or wasn't curious about the picture, which suited me just fine. I nodded. He drove off, flinging some sand my way.

Gillian said, "I saw George out the window. Mission accomplished?"

"He has the jar, and I have something else." I handed her the drawing.

She took it with both hands and looked it over front and back. "Nice!"

"I was so concerned about getting that in here without George seeing it that I didn't press him about what he said."

"What did he say?"

"There's been an attempted murder."

Chapter 11

"Not Mina?"

"I don't think so, Gillian. Surely, George would have said, considering he was here to pick up something she'd asked for. I keep forgetting that she's part of the club and, therefore, a target herself."

"The sooner we figure out what she's trying to tell us, the better. Although this drawing may help." Gillian frowned as she examined it. "I think I need a magnifying glass."

"I have a battery-operated one that lights up." I walked over to my desk and pulled out a large magnifying glass, brought it over to her, and flicked the switch on to demonstrate. "Remember to turn it off when you're through so the batteries don't run down."

"Perfect!" She sat down and began the examination. "Looks like Hepzibah is a composite, a persona used by anyone in the group. Which reminds me. I had some trouble pairing people with avatars until I remembered our conversation about these creatures being of two genders. I think I've got it now." She slid a sheet of paper across the table toward me. "I had Joe as the centaur because of his military service, but now I think he's the satyr because of his drinking. I think Amanda Glenn is the centaur because she's an award-winning horsewoman. The centaur looks androgynous to me."

I nodded as I looked over the list.

We both jumped at the knock on the door.

"That's probably Ricardo." I yelled, "C'mon in."

The door opened to admit Ricardo and Marc, talking as they entered.

"Hey! Marc has the reworked footage." Ricardo strode over to the table. "What are you guys up to?"

"This is what we wanted your help with." I pushed the lists toward them. "We're trying to figure out which characters go with which of the Triangle members to help us decrypt Mina's journal. The key to figuring out who the murderer is could be in there."

"Strikes me as a long shot," Marc said, picking up one of the lists.

"There's also this." I handed the picture to Ricardo. "Notice that the characters on this list," I tapped the paper Marc was holding, "are woven into the woman's dress in this picture that I took off the wall in Mina's house."

I pointed to the mermaid whose slender fishy form was part of the train at the back of the woman's gown. Both Ricardo and Marc compared the drawing to Gillian's lists.

Jack closed his computer and got up. "Want a beer, either of you?"

"Yes."

"Yes."

Jack headed toward the kitchen.

"We're trying to figure out if the kangaroo is a mythical figure in any culture. We're guessing at these relationships."

Marc looked up from the list. "And this is important how?"

"Mina had me retrieve the diary from her house and then told me to read it, indicating there might be something in here that could help us figure out who's trying to wipe out the club," I said.

"If that's what they're trying to do," Marc said. "There hasn't been anything on the news yet that would suggest that connection."

I frowned at him. "But you've been with us on campus. You were there. You know Mina."

He smiled. "I'm playing devil's advocate. People fall in love with their own theories. Challenge it. If it's the truth, it'll withstand inspection."

"I'll do that, but humor me for now. Help us look over what we've put together. See if you can find connections, reasons, anything. Mina's in a very vulnerable position."

Ricardo shook his head. "I know a lot about mythology, but no kangaroos. Sorry."

Marc shook his head, too. "No, but these others are interesting." He looked up at me. "The cops called me in for questioning again after the latest attack."

My heart jumped in my chest. "Who was attacked?"

He held up a hand. "Not Mina."

I exhaled. "Thank heavens. Do you know who?"

He nodded. "The new professor and she pretty much described me to a T as her attacker."

"But you didn't do it."

He smiled lopsidedly. "Thanks for that. No, I didn't, but I live alone and have no alibi."

"They let you go." Jack handed him a beer and passed the other to Ricardo.

"Yeah, they did, and I'm not sure why. If this were

a movie, they'd either have locked me up or followed me."

"Are you so sure you aren't being tailed? Plus, you have no motive," I said.

"That's certainly true." Marc took the list from Ricardo. "Some of these are the victims."

"They're the club members from the time Mina was in school here. From what she was saying, I think they tried to keep their membership to thirteen, which might mean that if someone graduated, they could be replaced. Are we looking at a bigger pool of people? A couple of members died before the reunion. In this diary that only covers one year of the time she was at school here, she assigns mythological creatures to each of the thirteen members of the club that she told me about. Except that we can't find a myth about kangaroos. And, yes, we've searched online. She has to mean something by it, but what?"

"Mina as a ghost. Interesting," Marc said.

"Remember, this diary was written contemporaneous to these members being on campus as students. They were probably different back then. For example, Mina's reserved now. She may have felt shy back then, that she wasn't seen, was as invisible as a ghost. Unless we have it all wrong, which is a possibility."

Gillian said, "Hi, George."

I turned to see her on her phone but looking at me.

"This is Gillian. I'm calling to find out how Libby is. We heard that she was attacked. Um-hmm. I see. Okay. Let us know if we can do anything." She clicked off. "Well, someone had to do it."

"And?" I said.

"Her wounds are superficial. He seemed reticent to discuss it."

"He's always reticent."

Marc raised an eyebrow at my comment.

"We dated in college."

He nodded. "I'm afraid I can't help with any of the others, but Professor Byrne may have been attacked because she's been around campus a lot, and the killer might have wanted to get her out of the way. You'll see from the footage that she's in the background of our shots quite a bit. You might want to consider putting her onscreen, maybe introducing the tour or something like that. She is a professor. She probably wasn't killed because she's not in the target group."

"Or maybe this isn't about the club specifically. Perhaps it's more about people who are on campus and make easy targets." Ricardo offered.

"All the other victims are decades older than she is," Jack said.

"She does live in the dorms, as do the club members, so currently, the campus is her home," Gillian said.

I pursed my lips. "There's just one thing. None of the club members or anyone else on campus, for that matter, looks like you, Marc."

"I know." He sighed, his brow furrowing. "Trust me, I know."

"Unless a student came back to get something he'd forgotten. Someone who lives in town, perhaps?" Jack said.

Ricardo shook his head. "The place is locked down tight now. I'm hoping we have enough to create the tour." He looked at Marc. "I know you want footage of the campus approach from the ocean taken by the drone, but I'm not sure we can get close enough."

"I'm confident we have enough footage now." Marc tapped the box he'd set on the table when he'd arrived. "If we can get more drone footage, that's a plus. I'm happy to do more work. Edits. Whatever. That is if I'm not in jail."

That dampened everyone's mood.

"Then we'd better have a look now." Ricardo pulled his laptop out of his backpack and loaded Marc's input into the software. "I'm going to cast this onto your TV."

Jack turned the set on, and some of us moved into the living room to be more comfortable. Up on the big screen, it was easier to see the details. We had more than enough footage, in my opinion. I made notes as we chatted about where to put the enhancements, what they would consist of, and who would voice them.

"This really looks good, Marc." My spirits rose. We could get this done on time.

"Was that a knock?" Gillian asked.

Marc paused the feed.

I set down my notebook and went to the door.

"Excuse me." George pushed past, scanning the room. "Marc MacKinnon, you are under arrest for the attempted murder of Professor Libby Byrne. You have the right…"

Marc paled but didn't say a word. He took a moment before he stood, walked around the end of the couch he'd been sitting on, and held out his hands toward George.

I saw the zip tie in George's hand, but I didn't hear the rest of what he said. My ears rang.

"George, this is wrong."

He paid no attention to me, zip-tied Marc, and took him out.

Marc looked back at us, his dark eyes vulnerable and pleading.

I yelled, "Don't say anything. I'll get you a lawyer."

And then they were gone.

"What the hell is he thinking? I can't believe I still love him." I noticed everyone was staring at me. "Did I just say that out loud?"

Jack cracked up. "Yes, Sis, you did. Too bad George didn't stick around to hear it."

Gillian grinned. "Told you so."

"I'll tell him." Doris materialized.

"Where have you been?" I asked.

Doris dusted imaginary dirt off her skirt. "Took a short trip on a rocket ship. The campus is open again. Not a copper in sight."

"Our videographer has been arrested."

"That cute guy? He wouldn't hurt a fly. What's your sweetie thinking?"

"Wish I knew, and he's not my sweetie."

She snickered. "I might not yet have materialized, but I heard you."

I threw my hands up. "Great. No privacy." My thoughts slipped and slid around each other. "I need to secure a lawyer for Marc. Mina will know someone. I need to get over to campus to talk to her. Thanks, Doris, for letting me know I can."

"They'll assign him a lawyer, or we can contact legal aid," Gillian said.

"This is wrong. Ricardo, I made some notes on that

pad." I pointed to where I'd left it. "I'll be back as fast as I can. I'm getting Mina a cell phone for Christmas. Will everyone be all right until I get back?"

Gillian said, "We'll be fine. You go make sure Marc will be okay."

"Wait a minute," Ricardo said, glancing down at the couch cushion recently vacated by Marc. "Marc left his personal stuff here."

"Wallet, keys, a couple of USB drives, and some folded papers." I was torn. "Gillian, can you grab a food container from the kitchen and put this stuff in it?"

Gillian nodded. "Sure thing."

"Stash it out of sight but don't obviously hide it. I don't believe safekeeping someone's possessions is illegal, but attempting to hide such from the police might be. I could be wrong. In any case, I've got to go see what I can do for him."

I grabbed my purse, jacket, and car keys and drove over as quickly as I could. Without a way to reach Mina except by searching for her, I knew I had to be fast. I was worried Marc would be scared. I was the first time I was questioned about a murder. Hopefully, he wouldn't say anything that might incriminate himself. Just my opinion, but cops could be pretty scary.

Mina was in her room.

"Hey! I'm glad I found you. I don't have much time. Marc has been arrested for the attempted murder of Professor Libby Byrne. I need to hire a criminal lawyer, stat."

Mina stiffened. "That explains our watchdogs' vanishing act. But that's not Marc."

"I know. Do you know someone local who can defend him well?"

Mina nodded. "In fact, I do. Sebastian Kane. He can be a bit gruff until you get to know him. He lives north of here on the other side of the point. Tell him I sent you. If you need his contact information, it's in the address book by my telephone in the parlor."

"Pretty sure I can find him on the Internet."

She smiled and nodded. "Of course you can."

I ran for my car and sat for a moment before starting it and did a quick search on my cell, found his office, and paused to consider that it was three days before Christmas. Oh, what the heck. I drove over. Not like it was that far.

His office was in a small California bungalow converted to offices two blocks off Main. A blue pickup sat in the parking lot. I hesitated, trying to decide if a lawyer would drive a pickup or if he was with a client, but I decided to give it a shot.

I walked up to the door and knocked. Out of the corner of my eye, I saw the curtain twitch aside.

A moment later, the front door opened, and a tall, thin man with graying temples looked me up and down. "May I help you?"

"Are you Sebastian Kane?"

He raised an eyebrow. "Yes."

"Mina Weber sent me. A friend of ours has been arrested for an attempted murder he didn't attempt. She said you were an excellent lawyer."

That drew a smile from him. "That much is true."

It was my turn to look askance. No lack of ego there.

"Will you help us?"

"You'd better come in. I prefer not to conduct business on my doorstep."

He stepped back, revealing no surprises in the waiting room. Leather couches and chairs provided comfortable seating. Bookcases lined the walls, filled with thick volumes. The room screamed: *This is serious business*. He closed the door.

"Follow me." He led me into his office.

As I sat, I noticed pictures of two teenagers framed and sitting next to each other on a cherry wood credenza. I wondered why he was working right before the holidays when he had a family to be with, but I was glad because I needed him now.

He pulled out a yellow legal pad and a pen. "Who was arrested?"

"Marcus MacKinnon. He goes by Marc. He's the videographer on a virtual campus tour my company is doing for Clouston College. He has no motive to hurt anyone."

Sebastian raised a hand. "We'll get to that. Your company?"

"CaRiMia." I spelled it. "We usually do website and promotion for local businesses. We're new. We only formed this year."

"Who's we?"

"Ricardo Santiago, Mia Howland, and myself, Cass—Cassandra Peake."

"You know for a fact that he was arrested in this town for attempted murder?"

"Detective George Ho arrested him in my living room. The murders were committed on the Clouston College campus."

"Murders?" His voice rose, and he looked up from his scribbles.

"You must have heard about it. Mirabella Ramos,

Sophia Pascarini, and Jonathan Alcott. They were killed on campus. They were there for a reunion of their club."

He leaned forward on his elbows. "I have, but you said an attempted murder. Please draw the lines between the dots for me."

"Sorry. There was a fourth person attacked, a new professor at the college who lives in the dorms until her condo is ready for her around the first of the year. Someone tried to kill her on campus, and she described Marc to the police as her attacker."

"The victim's name?"

"Libby Byrne."

He continued writing. "Had the professor met Mr. MacKinnon prior to the assault?"

"Yes, and Mina knows them both and is convinced that Marc didn't do it as am I."

He set the pad aside and spent the next fifteen minutes on his computer, neither speaking nor looking at me.

When I realized I was being ignored, I walked around his office, looking at his diplomas, pictures, books, and random papers lying around and getting an idea about who he was.

The pictures were the most interesting. In addition to the two kids I presumed were his, several pictures showed him with groups of men and women in suits in various locations. But the most interesting were the ones of him traveling with a lovely strawberry blonde. He looked very different, dressed casually with a smile on his face. I picked one up to examine it more closely and nearly dropped it when he said, "That's my late wife, Connie."

I set it back down hastily. "I'm so sorry. She's lovely."

"Yes, she is. I'll take the case. I have some papers to go over with you. My fee schedule, more direct contact info, items I'll need from you, and a few other things." He looked me straight in the eyes. "This is all contingent upon Mr. MacKinnon agreeing to my representation."

"Uh, yes, sure." I sat back down at his desk, and we went over the paperwork.

As I drove home, it struck me that it was remarkably easy to hire a lawyer. I felt elated at accomplishing the task. Then I thought about how Marc was going to pay him and panicked momentarily. The thought of Mina calmed me.

She wouldn't have suggested engaging Sebastian Kane's services if she didn't have a plan.

Chapter 12

I made a beeline for home.

"I'm starving." I hung my jacket on the hall tree. "Anyone else?"

Gillian stuck her head out from the kitchen. "We're in here having sandwiches and tomato-rice soup. Want some?"

I sniffed the air. My stomach growled. "Absolutely!"

Gillian had a bowl ready for me as I sat down. I picked up my spoon and ate for a few minutes before talking.

"We have a lawyer for Marc, but it isn't going to be cheap."

"I'll bet." Jack passed a plate of ham and cheese sandwiches to me.

I took two halves. "Sebastian Kane will talk to Marc, who has the final say as to whether or not to accept him as his lawyer. We'll see what happens, but I trust Mina. She sent me to Kane. She knows him."

"Does Marc have the wherewithal to pay for a lawyer?" Jack asked.

"I doubt it." I took a bite. "After all, he took this job with us while working a second acting job."

"How about setting up a funding page for him?" Gillian set a glass of ice water down in front of me. "Hydrate. We need to solve this. Only then will Marc and Mina be safe."

"I know. Someone is framing Marc, and we need to find out who and why. The police will try to prove he did all the crimes."

Jack said, "Who accused him?"

"Professor Libby Byrne."

"Why would she lie?"

"No reason that I can see. I figure she was confused and frightened. We're all a bit spooked." I finished the half sandwich I held and reached for the other part. "Can't believe how hungry I am."

"I've noticed how jumpy you are. Is there anything we can do?" Gillian put her plate in the sink. "Have you met all the club members? Do any of them resemble Marc?"

"No, I haven't met them all, but all the men are considerably older. Hard to make that kind of mistake. Although you make a good point. I doubt that Professor Byrne has met them all, either."

"We've recorded some news for you, and we've deciphered a few of Mina's stories," Gillian said.

Jack fetched his laptop from the dining room table. "Let's see. I was able to pull quite a few pictures off the Internet, given that most members have some sort of public life." He opened the file. "Milo Coates is way too short, which is why we think he's the leprechaun. Howard Castellano is a possibility. He's huge. Hmm. Jonathan Alcott was physically the closest, but he died before the attack on her."

"I still wonder about shadow guy and who he is," Gillian said. "From what I could tell at a distance, he was the closest physically to Marc. He might be the killer."

"Maybe he's a zombie," Jack said, enlarging a still shot from the video.

"Ignore him. Could a relative of one of the victims have been trying for revenge, not knowing that the professor isn't part of the club?" Gillian started to clear. "Want another sandwich before I put them away?"

I shook my head. "Believe it or not, I'm full. That's it for the men in the club?"

"Joe Pacenti is also dead but way before the reunion unless he didn't really die."

"How about sticking to helpful suggestions, Jack?"

Jack scanned the list. "Amanda Glenn is tall, dark, and pretty muscular for her age. She's the centaur, a horsewoman. She wears her hair up. I don't know the circumstances of the attack on Libby other than what they mentioned on the news, but Amanda's the closest physically to Marc among the women. She's nearly six feet tall with broad shoulders, but Marc has what…three…four inches on her? Can't tell the height of shadow guy from this shot."

"Eyewitnesses are notoriously unreliable," I said. "And don't make cracks about age."

Jack raised an eyebrow. "She's a lot older than you. She was a bit of a prodigy, so she was the youngest of the club members."

"You got all this off the Internet?" I tried to look at his computer screen, but he held on tight.

"You bet, and there's more. She inherited *beaucoup* bucks. She has a horse farm off 280 south of here."

"So, she's a local. Is she staying in the dorm?"

"Actually, she is. Bit of a surprise to me." Jack scrolled through the article. "Because she's used to luxury. You'd think she'd go home at night. I would, rather than stay in a dorm."

"Not really. If it were me, I'd want to be with everyone else. Isn't that the point of a reunion?" I turned the computer toward me. "I noticed that this group seems unusually close for being out of touch for so long. Maybe they haven't really been out of touch. Their lives have diverged, and yet all the living members turned up for this reunion, and they're all staying on campus, mostly in the dorms. They seem like an unlikely bunch."

"What holds them together?" Jack asked. "A criminal enterprise?"

I snorted. "I seriously doubt that. Can you see Mina involved in something illegal?"

"Maybe not before this, but now?" Gillian wiped the table, forcing Jack to lift his computer. Then she joined us. "How well do any of us know Mina? She always struck me as a bit mysterious."

Now that I thought about it, I agreed. I had no idea why I trusted her so much, but I did. I shook my head. "Not well, but I have faith in her inherent goodness. I can't tell you why, but mysterious or not, I'll do my best to prove her innocence. She's my friend."

Jack shrugged. "Okay. But where does that leave us?"

"The club is secretive. Mina gave us a journal from way back when, but it's in a kind of code. We think we've cracked the key, but so far, that hasn't been much help unless those stories you said you deciphered contain some clues. We have to clear Marc."

Gillian sipped her tea. "Any chance he did it?"

"No," I said before I gave it thought. I said more

slowly, "No. I really do not think he's involved in anything except working with us on the tour."

"He's an actor," Jack said. "Don't get me wrong, but actors act."

I shook my head.

Gillian said, "I was just throwing it out there. He doesn't have any motive, I can see. He's a really nice guy. But you could be on the hook for the entire lawyer's bill. You did hire him. You could lose your house. Be sure you know what you're doing."

She reinforced my own fears.

"I've come to the conclusion that I'm never sure what I'm doing. I didn't sign any papers, and I'm sure the lawyer knows I was contacting him on Marc's behalf. I told him Mina had sent me and that Marc was a mutual friend. But you're right. I do feel some responsibility, so trying to raise money for his legal fund is a great idea. Would you mind making me a cup of that tea? Feeling the need for caffeine."

Gillian smiled. "Sure thing. I'm sorry I threw that idea out there. I didn't mean to upset you further."

I shook my head. "Don't hold back. We need to think of everything. The answers are here somewhere. I don't want to keep interrupting the reunion, but I want to talk to Mina again as soon as I can now that Kane is engaged as Marc's lawyer." I took the cup Gillian handed me and warmed my hands on it.

"How long does this reunion last?"

"A better question is, will they let anyone leave until the murders are solved?" Jack asked.

"Christmas Eve is day after tomorrow. I'm guessing they'll all leave tomorrow at the latest," Gillian said.

"Something isn't right." I took a sip.

"That's an understatement," Jack said.

"I'm serious. We're missing something."

Gillian said, "You got Marc a good lawyer. You've done your part."

Jack looked over at me and smirked. He knew me too well. He knew I'd worry the problem like a rabbit with a carrot until I'd figured it out.

"Nope. I haven't done enough. Mina asked me for help, and she and Marc are friends. Somewhere in all of this are the answers we seek. Everyone on campus had opportunity, and I'd even say so did others. Although an empty campus means outsiders would be more conspicuous, like the shadow guy on campus no one could identify. I should show Mr. Kane that footage."

"Speaking of footage, are there security cameras on campus?" Gillian asked.

"I doubt it," I said. "I didn't see any, but more importantly, if there were, they'd know for sure that Marc didn't attack the professor."

"Or that could be why they arrested Marc," Jack said.

"I'll mention that to Mr. Kane." I tried to say it with aplomb, but a knot formed in my stomach again. "Means seem to be situational. But motive." I shook my head. "I just don't get motive. I might find a motive for one murder, but multiple murders of members of a decades-old club? Uh-uh."

"An old motive?" Jack said. "A decades-old one?"

"Who carries a grudge that long?"

"Loads of people."

"You, Jack?"

"Remember when you locked me in the tool shed

all afternoon?"

"You ratted me out to Mom."

Gillian held up a hand. "Let's drop the childhood grudge match. Point taken. Mina did nudge us in that direction by giving us an old diary, not a recent one."

"True. Can't believe you're still holding that against me, Jack."

"I'm not. It's just an example."

"Okay then. Given the age of the diary, I concede that the motive is probably an old one," I said. "That makes the attempt on Professor Byrne either an outlier or related in some way we still don't understand."

"I do have a spreadsheet set up, and information entered for the logical suspects, which includes the members of the Black Triangle Club, primarily. I've researched all of them. Want me to print out a couple of copies instead of all of us huddling around my small laptop?"

"Yes, please. We can look them over after I take a bio break. I'm going to make Christmas cookies tonight come hell or high water, but, Gillian, there's a small container of lemon bars in the freezer that need to be eaten. Could you take them out and let them defrost? Thanks."

Jack's eyes lit up. "Y'know, we've been light on the pizza this trip. We could order in, make cookies, and finish up decorating."

"Jack, that's brilliant!" Gillian kissed him on the cheek. "You call."

I headed to the bathroom.

Moments later, a rather disheveled Doris stepped out of the shower stall next to the toilet.

I screamed and tried to cover myself. "Privacy!"

Gillian knocked at the door. "You all right?"

"Yeah, it's just Doris, trying to give me a heart attack."

Gillian chuckled through the door.

Doris went all hands on hips. "*Just* Doris?"

I sighed. "You know what I mean."

"I'll forgive you if you let me stay to tell you what I found out."

I weighed my options. Knowing her propensity for practical jokes, I conceded defeat. "Sure. What've you got?"

"The reunionites are panicking. Everyone is packing and changing their travel arrangements."

"That's not good. We haven't figured out the real murderer yet, and I was hoping that they'd assume they were safe after Marc's arrest. Mina said the police had left the campus."

"Maybe that's why they're panicking." Doris shrugged. "Don't think it'll be an issue. From what I heard, it's cost-prohibitive to make a last-minute one-day change. You still have time to catch the killer."

"Can you leave so I can finish up in here?"

"Oh, sure." Her giggle was the last thing to fade away.

I processed what she'd said. If one of them was the killer, was that person fomenting panic in an effort to force a scattering of suspects? Were the members of the club turning on one another, or did they believe the attacks were coming from someone outside the group? Did they have any idea why they were being targeted? Was there guilt created by some escapades during their college days?

As I rejoined them at the trestle table, Gillian

asked, "Any news?"

"Doris says the reunion is breaking up. The members of the club are scared and want to head home but are having trouble changing their reservations. I thought she'd be out here with you guys. The locals can go home any time, of course."

Jack looked up from the computer. "That's weird. Don't they believe the murderer has been caught?"

"You'd think," I said. "I think they know something or have figured something out and suspect someone other than Marc. Their club was focused on research and problem-solving. I think maybe they've solved it."

"Why don't they go to the police?" Gillian asked.

"I don't know. Fear? I'm really torn about what to do. Should I go over there to try to find out what they know? Talk to Mina?"

"You could make her a target by singling her out," Gillian pointed out.

"Maybe it's time to talk to George," Jack said.

I startled at the knock on the door.

"See?" Jack said. "Jumpy."

As I opened the door, I said, "Good timing."

"I'm not even going to ask," George said, stepping across the threshold and hanging up his coat.

"I hesitate to say this, but why are you here?"

"I had a very interesting discussion with your cameraman, Mr. MacKinnon."

"You might as well join us in the kitchen." I led the way. "I'll only repeat what you say to me to Jack and Gillian, so you might as well tell all of us."

"Hi." George sat down across from Jack. "Under advisement from his lawyer, he told me about a volume of Mina's diary that you failed to mention."

So, Marc had accepted Kane's services. I thought quickly. I hadn't stolen it. Mina gave it to me. No law enforcement personnel had ever indicated that they were looking for said diary. Try as I might, I couldn't come up with any law I'd broken, although I knew I wasn't an expert. I put on the most innocent face I knew how.

"Diary? You mean Mina's journal? The one she asked me to get over the phone with you standing right next to her? Why would I mention it when you already knew all about it?"

His jaw clenched, and his eyes narrowed.

"Aw, c'mon, George, you know as well as I do that you weren't looking for any journal. Had you said you were, I would have mentioned it. We're happy to show it to you and explain what we've learned so far, which is pitifully little—"

"You're welcome to join us. We're going to make cookies, order in pizza from Clem's, and put up the rest of the decorations," Gillian said.

"C'mon, George, don't be a party poop," I said.

"Beer?" Jack asked.

The last of his authoritarian façade crumbled, and he laughed. "You're incorrigible."

"I try. I really do." I batted my eyelashes at him.

"You're trying. And I don't mean in a good way. Okay, if you'll show me the journal and tell me what you've learned so far, I can throw up a few decorations." But he smiled.

"Gillian, do you think the lemon bars are ready?"

She nodded and got them from the counter. "Let's move out to the dining room table. It's bigger. Shall I order the pizza? The usual?"

"Please. Thanks, Gillian." I led the way to the bigger table and produced the diary, handing it to George as he pulled out a chair.

Jack set up his laptop. George took the journal eagerly and thumbed through it. Then he frowned and paged through more slowly a second time.

"This is it?"

I nodded. "Now you see the problem and why we didn't suddenly have all the answers and come rushing to you with a solution?"

George sighed. "I assume you've made some headway."

Jack passed him a copy of the spreadsheet.

"Dragon? Mermaid? Seriously?"

I sat down next to him and gently took the journal. "Mina seems to have encoded all the entries. I haven't had an opportunity to talk to her to make sure we're on the right track, but I can tell you what we've surmised. You can confirm with her. I'd love to know if we're on the right track. We think the mermaid figure refers to Stephanie Bridges because she was on the swim team. Likewise, Amanda Glenn would be the centaur because she's an accomplished horsewoman."

I flipped pages until I found an entry about the mermaid swimming with others in the pond, observed by a djinn and an elf, with a drawing of a group of synchronized mermaid swimmers. "There's nothing in this story other than a memory that's probably about who was in the audience at a swim team event or water ballet, but there are lots of stories like this one. My assumption is that somewhere in here is the key to understanding the group's relationships and any conflicts that might lead to a motive for murder."

"Mina gave you this?"

"Yes."

"This is the diary she asked you to bring her?"

"Yes. Now, answer a question for me. Why are you still looking for evidence? You seemed pretty certain that Marc was guilty when you arrested him."

He shook his head. "There are a few things that don't add up. I'm pulling on the loose ends."

"That was nonspecific but hopeful," I said.

"You know I can't discuss the case with you in specifics."

"Well then, in generalities, do you think he's innocent?"

George sighed. "I'm following the evidence."

I yipped.

"Don't get too excited just yet. We still have to find something solid," George said.

Jack handed him a copy of the spreadsheet, notes, and the bios of the club members.

I gave him a chance to glance over the material before peppering him with questions. "Do you think it's a club member? Have you released Marc? Could it have been a woman who attacked Libby?"

He held up a hand. "Give me a minute to digest this." He ran his finger down our list of creatures. "These all relate to characteristics of the club members?"

"As far as we can tell."

He chuckled at Howard being a pooka. "I can see this. Hmm. Kangaroo. Not mythical as far as I know."

"We're puzzled by that one, too, but by process of elimination, that has to be Sylvan."

George shuffled the papers.

"What are you looking for?"

"Any stories about the kangaroo."

"Why focus on that one?"

"I always pull on the odd strings."

Gillian reached over and pulled out two of the pages of notes. "Here. Jack and I decoded a couple of stories with the kangaroo in them. I was curious, too."

George nodded at her and started reading. "Now, these are very interesting."

Gillian said, "Do you see it, too? Why she's a kangaroo?"

He nodded again. "I'm willing to bet the diary for the year before this one had her as a different character."

"I agree."

I folded my arms. "What are you two talking about?"

"What does a kangaroo carry in its pouch?" Gillian asked.

I gasped. "A baby."

Chapter 13

"There are few stories with Sylvan in them, and in the last one, the kangaroo hops away on an adventure. Jack and I went through the whole book. She vanishes."

Jack added, "She vanishes in real life, too. Our archive searches didn't turn up anything."

"Look for stories that are something other than college hijinks." George leaned back, eyes half-closed as if in deep thought.

"George, what are you thinking? We've been on campus filming. Maybe we've seen what you're looking for."

He exhaled. "What's the motivation for killing a bunch of retirees? Trying to find answers in an old diary is grasping at straws. A lot of time has passed."

Gillian, Jack, and I exchanged glances. "We came to the same conclusion about motivation. This is puzzling."

"Why is Mina leading you down a path to the past? Seems a bit suspicious." George's voice held an edge.

"Are you going to prevent the club members from leaving?" I asked. "One of them could be the killer."

George got up. "Now that you've given me the key to the code, I'm taking this stuff with me."

"That's it? Hit and run? *Again*?" I stood. "You did say you'd help decorate. We started without you." I'd known him too long to let him play the tough guy.

He tried to stare me down, but his mouth twitched. "Where are the decorations?" His voice was resigned.

We started decorating the tree. Tense at first, we got into it and got goofier as we uncovered some of the things Jack and I had made as children. Getting George to relax these days seemed harder than usual, and I wondered if it was because of the age of the victims. George had always had a lot of respect for his elders.

"No tinsel?" George asked.

"Nope. I have a cat who'll eat anything. That's why I have these." I pulled out the box of icicles. "Gillian's already hung a few. They're glass. Be careful and hang 'em high. Only unbreakable stuff on the bottom half of the tree. Thor is too big to climb this tree, but he has a long reach."

"You hope he can't climb the tree."

"I do, actually. Okay, you two are tallest, so you get the top half of the tree and all the breakable ornaments. Gillian and I will handle the cat-friendly section of the tree."

Just as George placed the star on the top, the doorbell rang.

"Pizza!" Jack headed for the door.

I stepped back to admire our work. "Beautiful! Did you know the Germans who came here brought Christmas trees into American culture?"

"Yes," said George. "Did you know that they also introduced the Easter Bunny? The Germans brought the concept of the Easter Bunny to the Pennsylvania Dutch area in the 1800s."

Gillian and I exchanged a glance. Was Mina's drawing a Pooka or an Easter Bunny?

"To me, the Easter Bunny and Santa Claus perform

a very similar function," George continued. "Cultural icons that treat good boys and girls. Behavior modification."

I frowned. "Santa has the naughty or nice list, but doesn't the Easter Bunny just dole out eggs and candy without asking questions?"

"Maybe now, but originally only good kids got colored eggs for Easter."

"In this house, good kids get pizza. Follow me." Jack led the way into the kitchen and set the boxes on the trestle table.

Gillian followed him and put plates and napkins down.

George looked around. "Did we get it all done?"

"Yes, we did." I dusted my hands off on my jeans and repacked the boxes with the packing materials to stash back up in the loft. "Would you mind hauling these up to my aerie?"

"No problem." George hefted the boxes as if they were feathers.

When he returned, I asked, "Are you sticking around for pizza? Maybe a little sleuthing?"

George laughed. "Sure...on the pizza." Then his smile faded. "I may get a call and have to leave. This case..."

I nodded. "I get it. Let's see how far we get."

We didn't question George about the case while we ate, but when he finished the last slice on his plate and reached over to thumb through the notes we'd given him, Jack pounced.

"Do you still regard Marc as a suspect?"

The corner of George's mouth quirked up. "You already know that we don't eliminate anyone until we have the person who committed the crime or, in this case, crimes. However, there now appear to be better suspects."

"The club members?"

George tilted his head and raised an eyebrow. "They are the most likely to have a reason to kill more than one member. Someone holding a grudge. We'll see if more information is revealed by this diary. Plus, we found what appear to be skin flakes on or around some of the victims. We're having them analyzed. Could be dandruff." He looked at our heads.

I reached up and touched my hair. "Most dust is composed of skin flakes."

He nodded. "Could be something not germane at all. Bad housekeeping. We'll know for sure soon. Mr. MacKinnon agreed to let our doctor check him out. He doesn't have any condition that would cause flaking. More serious skin conditions are largely something one develops as they age."

"That's not entirely true," Jack said

"No, but the odds are better."

"Pointing again to the club members as opposed to students," I said.

"Can you get DNA from skin flakes?" Jack asked.

George nodded. "A lot depends on the sample."

"And finding a match." Gillian stacked the plates.

"True."

"Can I talk to Mina about all this? Direct conversation with her would be so much easier," I said.

George hesitated.

"It would be much easier with her help."

"She could be the killer."

I shook my head. "She isn't. Trust me on this.

She's community glue."

"That doesn't preclude her being a murderer. Anyone is capable of murder if they feel justified."

"Nope. Not Mina."

He turned grim. "I'll have to ask you not to discuss any of this with anyone in the club. If you don't think you can do that, then you're barred from the campus until they're gone."

I thought about arguing with him further, but it was clear that wasn't going to get me anywhere. "So, we can return to film? I thought I could stay overnight in the dorms to catch the early morning light."

George narrowed his eyes.

"You said they were leaving…"

The corner of his mouth twitched.

"Have you released Marc? He could stay in the dorm as well to do the early morning filming and…provide some protection. I could get one of those things from the travel store. An alarm for the dorm door in case someone tried to enter in the night."

George rolled his eyes.

"I could get DNA from all the women," I said.

Jack said, "Wait a minute. George, you're the police. How can you ask my sister to do something you could do with search warrants?"

"Quiet, Jack. I want to do this." I waved him off. "Although that is a good question."

"First, I don't want her snooping around or doing anything suspicious like stealing things from anyone. Second, there is insufficient evidence for random warrants. We'd have to show we had the killer's DNA."

Jack narrowed his eyes. "But if you let her stay in the dorms, it begs the question are you trying to keep her occupied and out of your hair?"

"Another good question," I said, continuing to stare at George.

"You are a suspicious lot." He laughed.

I pursed my lips, trying to think of a retort. We couldn't film until Marc was out of jail. I did want to talk to Mina. Something was up with George that I wasn't privy to, but I had nothing to lose. A thought in the back of my head told me that wasn't entirely true, but I shushed it. George might be playing his own game, but I was still getting what I wanted if I could get him to agree.

"You said the killer was dangerous," Gillian said. "Are you putting Cass' life in danger by letting her go? If you believe the killer is living in the dorm, it doesn't seem right to place my sister-in-law in close proximity to a murderer."

"The killer is dangerous, and it would be foolish for you all to wander off randomly looking for him. I could get her a tracker and a second cell that links to us. Push one button, and you're connected. I'd check in with you repeatedly. I have a few other devices that'll help keep you safe, including a motion sensor for the door if you stay in the dorm overnight. You don't need to buy one."

"Wait a minute, why not use a police woman?" Jack asked.

Gillian said, "That's obvious, Jack."

"Cass has a relationship with Mina that many of them know about," George said. "The club members have already seen her. They know she's filming on campus. She's less suspicious than a stranger would be."

"Plus, I want to talk to Mina, and we do need to finish filming." I nearly crossed my fingers behind my back as I had as a child when I bent the truth.

"I do think most if not all will be leaving tomorrow, so there really won't be much of an overlap," George said.

Gillian nodded slowly. "It's the overlap you want, though, isn't it? No cleaning crew but no raised suspicions but locking down the area. You're letting the killer think they've succeeded. It's actually safer for Cass than it looks because the killer may drop his guard."

"Won't letting Marc go and then putting him into the dorm with them make the killer more suspicious?" I said.

"In or out?"

"In."

"Good." He stood. "I'll be back with your tools in the morning. Do not go to campus until you see me first. Thanks for the pizza." He held up the diary and the notes. "And for the info."

After George left, Jack said, "You can't do it."

Gillian said, "I agree with Jack. It's too dangerous, and he didn't answer your question."

"If you don't get a text from me every hour, come get me."

"Every hour? Sleep?" Jack asked.

"Am I not worth the loss of a little sleep? Besides, we won't know if this'll work until I go over and try to stay."

"I think it's a fool's errand. Nothing you gather is admissible in court." Gillian pointed out.

"That's true," Jack said. "Not properly collected.

What is it? Poisoned tree? Poisoned root?"

Gillian opened the dishwasher. "That's it. I'm cutting you off from those legal shows."

"I get it," I said. "But without any evidence, without a way to narrow the pool, the killer will go free. If they haven't killed all the people they want to here, they may pursue them to their homes."

"Where they might be more easily caught." Gillian pointed out.

"We have them all right here. This is the time to find out the truth."

"You just can't let it go and let George do his job, can you?" Jack said.

"I agree with you that he's not telling us everything. In fact, he was surprisingly chatty, but he's leaving things out. Something's definitely up. Part of me wants to go to keep track of Mina and make sure she's okay."

"She'd probably go home if you weren't going to hang out on campus. Can we at least try to narrow down the list a bit more?" Gillian said. "Let's put in some time tonight to give you as much information as possible before you move into the lion's den."

"Gee, thanks. Lion's den. But I would feel better if I knew more about the suspects."

Jack took a green and silver circle off his keychain. "Here. It's a small knife. Won't seriously damage anyone, but it might come in handy."

"Thanks." I slipped it into my pocket.

"What a Christmas!" Gillian said. "Jack and I will handle the Christmas dinner prep and the rest of it. Any idea what you want? Turkey?"

I brightened. "I have notes and a menu in the

pantry on the cookbook shelf for a big Christmas Eve dinner. Sitting right on top of the cookbooks. Recipes in the cookbooks have yellow sticky notes attached to the pages. Thanks, guys!"

"Let's focus on prep to keep you alive." Jack settled back down at the laptop. "Check the printouts. I'll update the file. You shouldn't take anything with you that might cause you to become the killer's target, so you'll need to familiarize yourself with all of this and remember it."

"No pressure."

"You can do it."

I pulled a copy of the printout toward me and picked up a pen. "If I have to memorize this stuff, we'd better get started." I read what we had. "There are six living female club members: Mina, Stephanie Bridges, Sentra Lee, Amanda Glenn, Mary Margaret O'Neill, and Tamsin Tredyffrin. It seems doable to get DNA."

"Don't you think it's going to be a bit difficult not to get noticed snatching drinking bottles, cups, hair from brushes, or gum?" Jack said.

"Prep, Sweetie, prep." Gillian poured him a glass of lemonade.

He sighed. "Right. Focus. I'm curious about whether or not these other characters that Mina has labeled can provide us with some other hints as to their personalities or characteristics. I don't think we've mined this diary for everything Mina meant us to find." He tapped the copies we'd printed out of the diary pages from our earlier scan.

"That's another reason I trust Mina. She's trying to help us and provide us with information that can solve these murders."

"I agree," Gillian said. "So, let's try to figure it out."

"If Sentra Lee is a dragon, what does that say about her? Look at the bio I pulled off the Internet." Jack pushed it toward me. "She runs her own import-export business. Does a lot of business with Asia."

"But that's now. Mina labeled her a dragon years ago." Gillian sipped her tea. "Want a cup?"

"I do. Thanks. Is she Asian? Could that be the reference?"

Gillian frowned. "Seems a little unsubtle, a stereotype even, but mermaid for Stephanie Bridges is pretty straightforward, too. Hmm."

Jack swung the laptop around. "Here's what she looked like back then. She was a debater."

I leaned forward. "Debating fiercely is more likely to be why she's a dragon. The characters are characteristics, not necessarily physical qualities, although we did tag Howard as a pooka because he's huge."

"But an Eastern dragon is very different from a Western dragon," Gillian said.

Jack continued. "Sentra has one daughter. Looks a lot like her. Divorced. Taking over the business."

"What've you got on Stephanie?" I asked.

"Athletic wear. Developed a line of clothing that moves and breathes with the athlete. She's still in pretty good shape." Jack frowned. "I think she's in a lot better shape than you are. She could be dangerous. Don't think "The Little Mermaid" story by Hans Christian Anderson. Think about mermaids that lured sailors to their doom."

"I thought that was sirens."

"No diff."

"If you say so. Next." I poised my pen over the paper.

"Amanda Glenn, the centaur. Now she's not in good shape. She's a socialite and all over social media. Rather heavier than when young. Ah. She has health problems that have made the news. She could have diabetes, given the charities she supports. She's local and has done some of the coordination for the reunion and the filming. I think we know the most about her."

"Or have a friend or relative with diabetes or simply be charitable. We can't afford to jump to a lot of conclusions," Gillian said.

"You might have to if you're going to survive this escapade. Three kids and four dogs. Rescues. The dogs, not the kids."

"I figured. Next."

"Mary Margaret O'Neill. Nymph or dryad."

"What's the difference?" Gillian asked.

Jack did a search. "Says here that dryads were tree spirits. Shy. Friends of Artemis. Different dryads inhabited different types of trees. Most were oak spirits. Daphnes inhabited laurels. Meliades lived in apple trees. Wow. That explains something. I think Mary Margaret was a dryad. Her daughter is named Melia."

I sat up straight. "Now that is interesting."

"And," he said. "They own apple orchards up in Washington State."

"Wow. A real tie from the past to the present. But check nymph just to be sure."

"Not quite so fast. The Meliae were the spirits of ash trees. That's confusing."

"Could be ash or apple, although the orchard

speaks to apple. How long has the family had the orchards?"

He nodded. "Generations. Apple it is. On to nymphs." He scrolled. "It seems we're dealing with classifications. Nymph is a category that includes dryads. Nymphs can inhabit trees, mountains, or seas."

"Okay, I don't think we have to worry that point any further. But we should make a list of children of club members. They're piling up. Next?"

"Tamsin Tredyffrin. Love her name. No idea how to pronounce it. She's the elf."

A bunch of elf images raced through my brain in rapid succession.

"Characterizing her is difficult. Can't find her under that name on social media, and yet with a name like that, I'd expect her to have a front and center type of career. Y'know, actress, magician, painter."

"You get all that from her name?" Gillian put the tea down in front of me.

I paused for a sip. "Let me look at those illustrations again. She looks like Galadriel. I wonder if she was into *The Lord of the Rings*? That might be all this reference means. She could have been a gamer."

"Possible," Jack said. "Nothing else really springs to mind."

I leaned back. "I have a lot to sift through."

"You're forgetting someone," Gillian said. "You do have to consider Mina even if you don't think she did it."

"The ghost," Jack said.

"I think that moniker refers to her being the unseen observer. The narrator. She always tells the stories. When I first met her, she talked about the ghost story books she's written." I sat up straight. "She's a writer!"

"So?" Jack asked.

"No, she's a ghost writer."

"Huh?"

"Haven't you ever wondered what she did for a living? How she affords a house out here on the coast?"

"You can afford a house out here."

"That's because mine actually came with a ghost. Seriously, I think Mina has ghost-written books for a living. It can be quite lucrative. It's not particularly germane to what we're doing now, but it certainly is interesting. Can't wait to talk to her about it."

"Focus," Gillian warned.

"Did any of that help us? Are there any hints in the composite character of Hepzibah?" I asked.

Jack shook his head. "We worked out the acronym for TRIANGLE. Truth, resilience, intellect, aspiration, nuance, giving, liberty, and education. Doesn't sound like a bad organization to belong to. Most of these six women have expressed those attributes in their lives. Several of the dead were educators." He leaned back in his chair. "Sorry to say, but they don't appear to be a very murderous bunch. What are we missing?"

"And yet so many are dead," Gillian said. "I do feel a bit better about you staying with this crowd."

"So, this exercise didn't reveal a killer, but I'm kind of looking forward to this. I'd like to get to know some of these women."

"No closer to our goal," Gillian said. "Not sure this augurs well for a quick resolution."

I stood. "I'm taking my notes up with me to study. I need some sleep. Can you guys lock up?"

Gillian picked up the tea cups. "No problem. You

go to bed. We'll handle it."

"Thanks."

I got a glass of water and headed upstairs.

Chapter 14

The next morning, I packed an overnight bag. That's all the time I would have before the club members left if they hadn't all taken off before now. Plus, I wanted to be home to celebrate with my friends and family, too. I had no idea what I would find upon arrival.

I dressed for comfort in cords and a Christmas sweatshirt. Kittens in stocking caps on navy. I regarded myself in the mirror. Pretty non-threatening. It would do. I laughed on the way down the circular stairs. In any case, I was mostly non-threatening.

The smell of coffee reached me before I hit the bottom step. And something else. Maple?

"Are you making pancakes, Gillian?"

"Already on the table and waiting for you. I like the sweatshirt. It's so not you."

"Thanks. I'm trying to look nonthreatening." I dropped the bag by the front door and headed for the kitchen, sniffing the air as I went.

"You're succeeding admirably. Kittens! Pancakes. Table. Eat."

I sat down, pulled the aluminum foil off the plate, and tucked in as if it were my last meal.

"Where's Jack?" I asked between bites.

She laughed. "He's not awake by any stretch of the imagination. He was up late worrying about you. I expect you to keep in touch; otherwise, you might get a rescue party when it's least convenient."

"I'll keep that in mind. If you get seriously worried, you can check with George." I took a sip of coffee. "Truth to tell, I'm a bit nervous myself. It seemed like a better idea last night." I took another pancake.

Gillian passed the maple syrup. "It'll be all right. Keep letting us know you're okay."

"I will." I wiped my mouth, took a last sip of water, and got up. "I'd like to get going. Where's George when you need him? Oh, and don't call my cell. I could be in the middle of something. Wait to hear from me." I hugged her as a yawning Jack emerged from his cocoon to see me off.

"Bye, Sis." He hugged me. "Take care of yourself and keep in touch."

"Will do."

Tires scrunched on gravel in front of my bungalow.

"Sounds like George is here."

I opened the door and let him in. "Got the stuff?"

He held up a bag. "Right here. Mr. MacKinnon is on his way to campus. I stopped at his place first and am delighted to say he's most eager to help."

"You mean you told him that if he didn't, he might wind up back in a cell."

"That, too."

But as I was about to explode, I saw the twinkle in George's eye. "You can be very irritating."

"Just trying to live down to your expectations."

He went over the equipment and let me know that they should be able to find me very quickly if I signaled that I was in trouble.

He walked me to my car and tossed my bag in the back seat. "Do not hesitate to call me if there's any sign of a problem."

His intensity gave me pause.

The breeze ruffled his short hair, and he hugged me. "Drive safely."

"I will."

As I pulled out onto the street, I looked back. George watched me as I drove away. What was he thinking?

Once on campus, I parked in the lot behind the dorm and went to look for Mina, but her room was empty. Her suitcase was still in the closet. I took the opportunity to pull some hair out of her brush and stuff it into a plastic baggie I'd brought with me. Then I put my suitcase in her closet so that she'd notice it if she planned to leave and shut the door. I put a couple of baggies in my pocket. Then went to look for her.

I found five of them in the lobby lounge area, sitting in armchairs covered in brightly colored fabric, chatting. Set up for four to a wood block coffee table, the aesthetics were thrown off by someone who had pulled another chair over. I went through my mental list of members, seeing their pictures in my mind's eye. Milo stood when I entered the room.

"Can we help you?"

Sentra looked up. "You're Mina's friend." She'd twisted her hair up and held it in place with ornate enameled red wooden chopsticks.

"Yes, I was looking for her. Do you know where she is?"

"Maybe she went with Amanda and Stephanie," Tamsin said.

"Do you know where they went?" I asked.

Milo said, "Mina's not with them. Amanda drove Stephanie to her doctor and then to Amanda's home. Stephanie woke up with shingles. She's in terrible pain. Fortunately, there are meds they can give you now. Steroids and antivirals. She'll be okay."

"Broke up the party," Tamsin said. "Although it's probably time we all went home."

"It is a little unusual to hold a reunion during the holidays. Most people travel to see their families," I said.

Tamsin's aging beauty softened features that looked sharp in photos. She still had long, thick hair. "You'll understand when you're a bit older. Do you have any children?"

I shook my head. "Not yet."

She nodded. "Some of us are estranged from our children. Some of us are alone and childless." She gestured dramatically with her arm. "And what other time of the year could we have an entire college to ourselves?"

Milo coughed, drawing everyone's attention to him and away from Tamsin. He was a bit of a sparkplug. "Join us while we wait for Mina, won't you? We're all going out to dinner tonight. Last night of the reunion. In the meantime, we thought we'd round everyone up for a bit of lunch and reminiscence at Melon-choly. You know the place?"

I nodded. "The fruitarian restaurant. I like Callie's Flower better. More variety. They include veggies." I realized he still stood. "Thanks for the invite." I sat.

"You're welcome to join us for dinner later if you'll be around," Mary Margaret said. "I don't think we've met. I'm Mary Margaret O'Neill. You must know about our little club if you're a friend of Mina's."

"I've only known Mina for a short time. I moved here from Pleasanton after my divorce. She was the first person I got to know."

"Did she ever tell you about us?" Howard asked.

I shook my head. "Not until this reunion. Even now, we haven't talked because she's been here with you."

Marc walked in. "I thought I heard voices."

"You're the guy with the cameras," Howard said.

"That's me. Cass and I," he nodded toward me, "have a few more shots to catch in the early morning light. We thought maybe we could stay here tonight and shoot in the morning."

Sentra narrowed her eyes as she looked at me. "So, not here for Mina."

I quickly corrected her. "Yes, I'm definitely here to talk to Mina, but Marc is also correct. We have very little left to film. The murders got in the way of our completing the video." As soon as I said it, I knew it was insensitive.

There were looks all around, and the atmosphere chilled. I prayed I hadn't just blown it.

Milo looked at his watch. "Mina's late. Hate to go eat without at least asking her if she wants to come."

"Any idea where she went?" I asked.

"I think she must have gone out," Howard said. "She told us she walks every day."

Funny, I'd never noticed that. What I did notice was the black cat sitting quietly in the corner of the room under a small table next to a comfy leather armchair. I swear Thor smiled at me. Thoris! Doris had forced my cat all the way to campus. It must have taken her hours. I felt comforted to have her here.

"Should we go looking for Mina? It's chilly out. She might have fallen." Sentra turned to me. "She's your friend. What to come along? You might not want to stay here alone."

I locked gazes with Marc, wondering if she meant something by that, and I shivered. Were they thinking the same thing I was? Had the killer gotten her?

"Maybe we should call the campus cops," Milo said in his low, gravelly voice. "We don't know for certain that she is taking a walk."

"Good idea." Mary Margaret stood, pulled out a cell phone, turned her back on us, and called them. A few minutes later, she rejoined us. "Sorry, but I don't think this is the time to be coy. We need to stick together, or whoever is doing this is going to pick us off one by one."

"You think the killer has Mina?" Tamsin said.

"I think it's a distinct possibility." Mary Margaret tucked her phone in her pocket.

Cold chills ran down the backs of my legs.

Robbie entered the lounge, looking official, his hand resting on his sidearm. "What's the problem?"

Mary Margaret took a step toward him. "I'm the one who called. Mina Weber is missing. We think she might have gone for a walk and hasn't returned. We were all going to get some lunch and wanted to include her. We're afraid she's fallen or..." Her voice shook.

"Stay here." Robbie stalked out, talking on his radio.

I glanced across the room, but Thoris was gone. I looked back at the group. Most of them seemed to be sincerely worried about Mina, but Tamsin had suggested that she might already be a victim. They were all here and had been together waiting for Mina. I shook my head. The killer couldn't be among them. That left Mina, Stephanie, and Amanda. Did Stephanie really have shingles? Were she and Amanda in cahoots? Had they taken Mina off somewhere in the woods to kill her? Or had one of this group left, ostensibly to go to the restroom or to a room to fetch something, and engaged in a touch of homicide on the way?

I couldn't sit still any longer. "We need to tell Robbie about Stephanie and Amanda."

Milo looked up. "He knows. He escorted them to Amanda's car."

"So, he knows that Mina didn't go with them," I said.

"She wouldn't have agreed to meet us for dinner if she'd planned to go with them," he said.

"True."

Visions of Agatha Christie danced in my head, and I briefly wondered if they were all in on it. But reality struck quickly. There was no reason for the club to cannibalize itself. None that I could see, anyway. It just made no sense. Unless this was all innocent, and Mina had really just twisted an ankle somewhere.

"But I can't stand still and wait."

Marc joined me, his tall presence reassuring. "We could look for her."

A chilling thought occurred to me. If Mina were the only member of the club not accounted for, I had to consider that I'd been totally wrong. That she was the killer. I thought about what I knew about her from the day she'd sat in my dusty kitchen right after I'd bought the bungalow, looking around the room, spooked by the possibility of encountering the ghost that she'd helped to conjure, to the day she'd provided us with her old college diary with its entries about the club to help us solve the murder. Had that been a ruse? Something to throw us off her trail? A red herring?

I had to know. "Yes," I said. "But where do we start?"

"We could leave it up to the campus cops and go to lunch." Milo stood again and looked around at the group. "Or there are some possibilities inside the buildings."

Howard rose also. "The campus cops are handling the outside."

I pressed a button in my pocket. It would record even if it couldn't transmit right away. I remembered what Mina had said about secrets and steam tunnels. If we were going somewhere secret and potentially underground, I was afraid George wouldn't find us.

A little more reluctantly, Sentra, Mary Margaret, and Tamsin stood.

Mary Margaret said, "I don't suppose I'd have any luck trying to persuade you all to go to lunch?"

Tamsin shook her head. "We'd look for you if you were missing."

Mary Margaret sighed. "Lead on, Milo. You were always the explorer."

Marc and I took up the rear as Milo and Howard led the way to the bowels of the building. If I was wrong about Mina, we could be walking into a trap.

Everyone was silent as we descended into the abyss. We hadn't stopped for any equipment. I felt in my pocket for the little circular knife. I had a flashlight on my cell phone, but I wondered if we'd be stumbling around in the dark.

Milo flipped a switch at the top of a narrow flight of stone steps that led down into darkness. Nothing happened.

"Howard?"

"I'll get it." Howard vanished into the darkness.

There was a clang in the dark that made me jump.

"Ow!"

"You okay, Howie?"

"Barked my shin."

After several clicks, Howie's voice echoed out of the blackness. "Try it now."

Milo flipped the switch again, and a pale glow emanated from beneath us.

I inhaled sharply.

Marc whispered, "It'll be okay."

I nodded, and we followed them down into the pit. The heat increased as we descended. At the bottom, we turned down a passageway and shimmied past huge, hot steam pipes. Howard and Marc had the most difficult time moving through without getting burned. Sentra's body seemed to bend and slip around the encumbrances most easily.

Periodically, we went through "doors" that were merely hinged pieces of wood that didn't keep out the small, scurrying animals. I looked around at the foundation in these areas and decided the doors must demarcate the edge of buildings or sections of buildings. I wondered if it was a way to know where you were. I was already horribly lost. If I hadn't been with others who seemed to know their way, I'd have been afraid that I'd be wandering down here forever and starve or learn to eat raw rats like Thor. I wondered again where Thoris had gone. Where was my ghost taking my cat?

Then I noticed the markings on the walls. Most were faded, but some of the old ones were still legible.

"What the hell?" Milo exclaimed and stopped, causing a bit of a pile-up.

"What is it?" Howard's voice rose above the annoyed grunts.

"Someone's been down here and recently. Some of these markings are profane." Milo pointed to a few.

"Just a new crop of students, Milo. We knew it would happen eventually."

A hush fell over the group as we all passed the new signs, some of a peculiarly phallic nature. We were single file now, and Marc brought up the rear. I looked back to see the dark close in behind him as we advanced.

"We're here," Mary Margaret said, her voice hushed.

Where?

Something furry scurried past my ankle. I didn't look down.

The door stuck, but Howard threw his considerable bulk at it, and it gave way with a loud bang as it hit the inside wall. Someone screamed.

I was still out in the hall and couldn't see a thing. Tension emanated from Marc. Whatever was in the room, I wasn't sure I wanted to see it. The pressure on the crowd lessened as people entered silently. As I reached the door, I understood why.

Across a storage room full of old equipment, decaying cardboard boxes collapsing in stacks in the corners, cobwebs, mouse skeletons, and piles of dirt and other stuff I wouldn't want to examine more closely, stood Mina, tall and silent.

I guessed her posture was at least partially due to the large chef's knife pressed against her throat.

The woman holding it trembled. "Stay back."

"Professor Byrne?" I said.

"Not for long," Marc whispered in my ear.

"Finally. Some answers. Get in here. All of you. No, no! Stop, Marc. I saw you. No one gets out of here until I get some answers." Her voice shook, not with fear but with anger.

Sentra stepped forward, the smallest among us. "What do you want to know?" Her voice was as smooth and silky as her long, black hair.

"What did you do to my mother?"

Mina focused on me. Perhaps I was reading too much into that look, but it made me even more determined to get her out of here in one piece. At first, I'd wondered why Milo led us down here, but I realized he thought Mina might be here because the club had come down here often, probably to meet privately. It might have seemed exciting to young college students. The room grew claustrophobic as we all moved around the walls, keeping our distance from Libby Byrne.

"Who's your mother?" Sentra took a step forward.

"Stop right there! This club took a vow to always be there for one another. To always come to each other's aid. You broke that vow!" She spat the words, much as a snake spits venom.

Sentra froze. "Your mother was a member? But we're all—"

"Must be Sylvan. We know each other's children.

She even resembles her a little now that I think of it," Mary Margaret said.

Sylvan must have been a knockout. I remembered my first impression of this woman.

"She's the only woman in the club who died before this week," Tamsin said.

"Is she dead? How did she die?" Libby Byrne's voice shook. "Who among you killed her? By not helping her, you all had a hand in her demise." She tightened her grip on the knife.

Mina winced as a thin trickle of blood ran down her neck.

Sentra raised her hand toward Mina.

"No," Tamsin said slowly. "Why don't you know what happened to your mother?"

"We were living in Manila."

Mary Margaret said, "I thought she went to Nepal."

"She did but decided to have me in a hospital in Manila. She thought it would be safer. Did she contact you? Did she ask for your help when she found out she was in trouble? Did you ignore her?"

"That doesn't sound like Sylvan." Sentra frowned, turning first to Mary Margaret for confirmation and then back to Libby. "How do you know she had you in Manila? You weren't born yet."

All the whispered conversations stopped.

"I…"

Her hand wavered, and her eyes darted from one to another of us. Then her grip on the knife strengthened.

"I have a letter from the consulate from when I was sent to the States."

Sentra tried again. "What makes you think we had anything to do with whatever happened to your mother?"

"Why did you let her leave, knowing she was going to have a baby? You swore to protect her."

"You never knew your mother, did you? It was impossible to make Sylvan do anything she didn't want to do. She was the ultimate free spirit," Sentra said.

Tears started down Libby's face, and the air seemed oppressive. "She wrote about how close you all were. How you could rely on each other. How you would change the world. She wrote about your rituals. Raising spirits. Ritual magic." She pointed to once bright but now faded painted circles on the floor. "The evidence is right here."

I got the creepy feeling she wanted us to raise her mother's ghost to get her answers.

Apparently, Sentra came to a similar conclusion. "We are not holding a séance down here."

Libby's lips thinned. She pressed the knife tighter against Mina's neck, drawing fresh blood that ran in a thin line to the collar of her dress and spread into a diffuse half-circle as it met the gauzy lilac fabric at the neckline.

"Okay," Tamsin said. "Séance it is."

That earned her a swift and dirty look from Sentra.

Tamsin returned the look, holding her arms out, hands upraised in a what-else-would-you-suggest pose.

Mina remained still as stone. Everyone else started to move slowly about the room, looking for anything to aid them. Libby watched everyone carefully, maintaining her grip on the knife. Marc and I stood near the door and didn't interfere. Even though I had some experience now with séances, I assumed they had their way of doing things.

Some of their *accoutrements* appeared to have been stashed in boxes in this room, and I wondered again what they had gotten up to down here when young.

When ready, they formed a circle as if they had been doing this sort of thing all along. Four of us remained along the outside, and the five of them stood at the hastily drawn points of a pentacle. They held hands and began to chant.

This was proving to be a very different sort of séance than I was used to.

Their hands moved up to their shoulders, and they leaned in, never breaking the chanting. Now they swayed from side to side. The room was already hot, and the swaying and chanting had become hypnotic. The amount of energy being generated was electrifying.

Libby appeared dazed, and her hand dropped just slightly. Mina glanced down at the knife. Then a large, black cat leaped onto Libby's head from a pile of nearby boxes. Gray mist bled over the professor, who screamed, dropped the knife, and clawed at the haze.

I lost track of Thor in the ensuing melee.

Mina sidestepped out from under Libby's grip and ran to us. Milo tackled Libby, who hit the ground hard. The gray mist vanished, dissipating either into Libby or the thick, steamy air. Libby continued her shrill ululation for a moment. Then her cries turned to sobs as she thrashed from side to side.

Marc grabbed Thor by the scruff of his neck and picked him up. Oddly, Thor didn't protest but went limp.

I pushed past the others and tried to take Thor from Marc. He stopped me.

"He's heavy. I'll carry him. Don't worry."

I put my hand on Thor's flank to reassure myself that he was still breathing.

"Thanks, Marc."

We were a solemn group as we marched back through the narrow passage and up the stone steps with Howard on one side and Milo on the other, holding Libby up and guiding her along, although she appeared not to care any longer. She sobbed quietly as she allowed them to lead her. When we emerged from the sub-basements to the ground level, the phone in my pocket vibrated. We had connectivity again.

Sentra had also noticed and had her phone to her ear in seconds. We all traipsed back to the lounge: the nine of us plus Thor. Libby collapsed on the floor, and no one made an effort to help her to one of the chairs.

I sat down next to Marc and stroked Thor.

A tall woman in a perfectly tailored scarlet suit rose from a chair. A streak of white cut across the front on her short, dark hair.

"Did I miss all the fun?"

Sentra stepped forward. "Sylvan?"

Libby's head jerked up. "Mother?"

Sylvan looked down at her daughter. "Liberty?"

The doors banged open, and Robbie, accompanied by another member of his team, George, Rusty, and Bill piled into the room. Robbie scowled at us but deferred to the town police.

George and Bill helped Libby, who was crying and struggling toward her mother, up and read her rights as they handcuffed her.

Rusty, efficient as usual with her auburn hair neatly done in a French braid, blocked Sylvan's attempts to get to her daughter. Bill took Libby out as Rusty and the two campus security guards moved around behind the rest of us.

"I'll need statements and contact information from all of you even if you've supplied it already." Then George smiled. "You can go ahead with your plans to leave tomorrow to spend the holidays with your families once I have those statements. The officers will provide you with the forms. Don't leave this room until you've returned them to one of us."

"Or you are welcome to stay at my house for the holidays." Amanda stood in the doorway. "Stephanie is responding to the drugs the doctor gave her but is staying through New Year's to recover a bit before journeying home. Both she and I want you all to come. You left us out of the adventure!"

The group swirled around Marc and me, talking at once as the tension in the room eased. They'd somehow remained close despite the passage of time. Quite the group. Not at all what I expected at the beginning. They quieted down as each was given a form and sat down to fill them out. All but Sylvan, who was talking animatedly to George.

Rusty handed forms and pens to Marc and me. Thor didn't stir as Marc shifted him so that he could fill out the paperwork.

Mina came over to Marc and me and hugged us.

"Thank you, Cass. I knew you could find the answer." She looked over at Sylvan. "If only she'd arrived earlier."

"Or contacted the daughter who killed three people while looking for her!" I shook my head.

"There's always more to the story." Mina patted my hand.

"We searched the Internet and newspaper archives for Sylvan Woodbright and never found a whisper of her."

"From the ring on her finger, I'd say her name isn't Woodbright any longer."

"That's quite a rock," Marc said.

"I tried to get Libby to let me go, and she did a bit of talking down in the tunnels. When she tried to ask Mirabella about Sylvan, Mirabella guessed who she was. Apparently, I wasn't the only one who knew Sylvan was pregnant. Libby almost lost her fight with her. Mirabella was a fitness nut and very muscular. Libby is younger and healthy, but she wasn't a match for her. In the end, she knocked Mirabella off balance, and when she fell on the equipment, Libby hit her with a weight. I think that's when she realized we might be her best source of information."

"Still, why not hire a detective to locate her mother or find out what happened to her?"

"She did, but she's not a wealthy woman. She lost out on the job here, and her money ran out. Libby spent her savings on her quest for the truth about her mother. She thought her luck had changed when the position became available and the school needed a replacement quickly. They had already vetted her because she'd been a finalist for the position when Professor Stone got it instead. When she heard about our reunion, Libby contacted the college and took the job immediately. She planned to simply talk to us, but Mirabella's death, then Sophia's arrogant hostility pushed her down a different path, unfortunately. She did skewer Sophia with her own cane sword. Sophia was frail and had osteoporosis—an easy target—but I'm willing to bet

Sophia attacked with her tongue. I believe you experienced it. By the time she got to me, Libby was desperate."

"I'm glad we made it in time."

"As am I."

"I stashed a bag in your closet. I'd planned to stay here with you and Marc and do some pickup shots in the morning, but I'd really rather go home if George lets me."

Mina smiled. "I understand. I think we'll all be fine now. I also think most of us will take Amanda up on her offer. I would like to spend more time with my old friends rather than going home alone after... And Amanda's place has to be more comfortable than these dorms."

I hugged her. "I'll see you when you get back."

Mina moved off to be with her friends.

"Let's go talk to George," I said.

Marc shifted Thor to one arm as he stood.

George took his equipment from us. "Why don't you both go back to Cass', and I'll meet you there when I'm through here. I will have to get formal statements from you both."

Marc held up a finger. "I need to check that I'm no longer under arrest, nor am I a suspect. After you get what you need from me, I will have met my obligations to you."

George smiled, looked down at his feet, and then back up at Marc. His eyes twinkled. "You are not currently a suspect in any criminal matters under investigation by the Las Lunas police. You are to be commended for your service to the department, and aside from needing to provide a formal statement, you are free to go."

I didn't have to be told twice. I waved to Mina. She and several others waved back.

Marc walked me to Mina's room to get my bag and then out to the car.

"You can put Thor on the back seat."

"I'll bring him and be right behind you." He pushed my car door shut.

I drove home in a bit of a daze.

Jack and Gillian were surprised to see me, and I collected two hugs.

"Where's Thor?" Gillian asked.

"Marc's bringing him. He should be here soon. I'm very, very thirsty."

"What happened?" Gillian asked.

I related the whole story while she reheated leftovers for me. It felt so good to be home in my bungalow, but uneasiness plagued me. Where was Doris? I'd half expected her to be here.

Maybe a shower after those steam tunnels would make me feel better.

Chapter 15

Jack answered the knock at the door and let Marc in.

"Did Cass get back safely?" Marc asked as he stepped over the threshold.

"She's in the kitchen, wolfing down food. There's plenty to eat if you're hungry." Jack closed the door. "She'll be very happy to see him." He nodded toward the huge black cat in Marc's arms.

As Marc laid a very limp Thor on the couch, I hurried over to check on him.

"He hasn't moved a muscle since I picked him up, but he's still breathing. You may need to take him to the vet tomorrow." Marc straightened up. "I'm starving."

He hung up his jacket and followed Jack into the kitchen.

"Thanks for bringing Thor home. Have a seat." I gestured toward the pizza. "Help yourself."

He did, digging into a slice of leftover pepperoni pizza before his seat hit the chair. "Um. Good."

Having Thor back only answered half my worries. "Gillian, has Doris come home?"

She shook her head.

"We haven't seen her." Jack turned to Marc. "Beer?"

"Please. Who's Doris?" He took another slice.

171

"Ah…" My mind raced. Had we not told him about Doris? Had he never met her?

Gillian, Jack, and I exchanged glances.

Marc's eyes narrowed. "You're right, Cass. You're not an actress."

He said it kindly but with a bit of steel in his voice. Until now, I'd thought he was pretty easygoing.

"Oh, didn't I mention Doris?" I tried to sound innocent as if it were no big thing.

"No, you did not. I repeat, who's Doris?"

Jack said, "Just tell him."

Gillian nodded. "Don't think you have a choice, and I think he can handle it."

"Wow, Doris must be one tough cookie." Marc took the beer Jack handed him.

"You might want to take a long pull before she tells you," Jack said.

Marc took his advice, set the beer down, and placed both of his hands flat on the table. "Ready."

I took a deep breath. "Doris is my ghost."

He raised an eyebrow. "Metaphorically speaking?"

"I'd hardly be waiting for a metaphor to come home."

"No, I suppose not. But having acted in a number of low-budget local horror films, I do know a bit about ghosts. It isn't standard operating procedure for a ghost to be able to wander far from its haunting ground."

I nodded. "That's true for Doris."

He frowned, looking perplexed. "Then why are you waiting for her to come home? And why worry about a ghost? Most people want to get rid of them."

I scrunched my eyebrows together. How to get out of this tangle? "You brought my cat home."

He nodded.

"He was down in the steam tunnels and attacked Libby."

"True."

"Did you see the gray mist?"

"Yes," he said a little less certain this time.

"That was Doris. She can inhabit Thor or other small animals and leave the premises. However, if she leaves Thor without another host…" My voice broke.

Gillian put her hand on my shoulder. "We don't know what might happen to her."

Today had been too much. Tears ran down my cheeks.

I spoke on a sob. "She left Thor to attack Libby and save us, but Thor wasn't anywhere near her when she would have needed to return. I didn't see anything else she could have inhabited. I'm worried about her."

"You're serious." His voice sounded surprised.

"As a heart attack," Jack said. "Which Doris frequently tries to give me."

"Sometimes it takes her a while to get home, depending on her ride," Gillian said.

"I know. I'm just worried."

"Her ride?" Marc said.

"It could be anything," Gillian explained. "From a mouse to a bird to a cat or a rabbit." Gillian chuckled. "Doris says some are a bit harder to steer than others."

Marc finished his second slice. "There must be mice in those tunnels. I hope she got out. I'd like to meet her."

He seemed sincere.

There was a second knock at the door, and Jack went to let George in.

"There's still some pizza, George," I called out from the kitchen. "You didn't really want DNA, did you?"

"Hi, Marc," George said as he strolled into the kitchen.

"Huh, you didn't call him Mr. MacKinnon. By the way, I do have a baggie of Mina's hair that I took from her brush. Nothing else, I'm afraid. Things started to happen rather quickly after I arrived. Libby had already taken Mina."

George smiled. "The recording will do just fine. Thank you." He turned to Marc. "Would you prefer to be called Mr. MacKinnon?"

Marc shook his head. "No, absolutely not. Marc is just fine. Thank you very much."

That made me laugh. "I guess that means you're friends. George, can Marc call you George?"

George raised an eyebrow and looked straight at Marc.

Marc raised both hands and shook his head. "Not necessary, sir."

George laughed. "Call me George. Any friend of Cass'…" He looked at me. "Your little escapade has wrought changes in the college already. Robbie told me he'll be installing more impenetrable barriers down in the steam tunnels and maintenance areas now that he's more aware of what shenanigans students can get up to."

"*My* escapade?" I laughed. "That pig is already out of the pen. Speaking of pigs, I need a shower…badly."

"I'll bet. Although it was probably less hot down there than usual. The techs won't appreciate that, though, as they pore over that maze, looking for evidence."

"It's creepy down there, too. Full of things that slither and crawl." I shivered.

"Sounds delightful. Robbie says the student handbook calls out possible expulsion for those who venture into the nether regions."

"It doesn't call them the 'nether regions,'" I said.

"Restricted areas, I believe."

"I just realized something else."

"What?"

"The college will need a new folklore professor…again. Was that woman really her mother?"

George took the beer Jack offered him. "You mentioned shooting more footage?" He turned to Marc. "I'm afraid that won't be possible."

I looked over at Marc, too. "Drone?"

He smiled. "We wanted to use Ricardo's drone to get footage of the college as the drone approached campus from the ocean. Do you mind if we stay on the periphery or maybe down by the planetarium and shoot for, oh say an hour? If not, we do have enough. It was more of a cover story so that we could spend the night in the dorm, but it would be great footage for the tour."

George pursed his lips, but he nodded. "Okay. I think we can allow that. Give me time to let them know."

"No problem. Now, if you all are through with me, I can go over to Maya and Theda's, and we can get to work on it." He looked around at all of us. "This has been quite an education. Keep me posted, Cass."

"Will do."

"Not so fast. I need the camera again," George said. "Sorry."

"I understand." Marc passed his camera bag over to George. "Please be gentle with my equipment. It's expensive. I need a receipt."

George wrote out a receipt and handed it to him. "Thanks for being so cooperative."

"No problem. I know you're just doing your job." Marc remained standing but stuffed his hands in his pockets.

George eyed him suspiciously. "You can both come down to the station in the morning. Ten o'clock. I want to look through the footage and listen to your recording before I take your statements for the record. You can get your camera back then. I want this tied up with a nice, big, red Christmas bow." George stood. "See you then, and thanks for the beer."

"Tomorrow is Christmas Eve," I protested. "And you didn't answer my question!"

He ignored me as he picked up the camera bag and left.

When he'd gone, I relaxed a bit. Turning to Marc, I said, "You were later getting here than I expected."

"I anticipated George and pulled into Maya and Theda's, uploaded all the footage, and left all my equipment except for the camera I used last on-campus that he saw me with. I had a feeling he'd take them again. I'm learning."

I sighed with relief. "Then we really are good to go."

"Yes, we are. Thanks for the snack. I'm going to go get started. This job with you has been one wild ride. Let me know if you ever need my help again, though. Very exciting."

I showed him out. "Will do."

Jack and Gillian sat down at the table with me. "Home for Christmas now?"

I frowned. "It's not over yet. I have several unanswered questions. Was the woman really Sylvan Woodbright? Where's she been all these years? Why did she show up for the reunion? Why didn't she reclaim her daughter or at least contact her?"

"Cookies?" Jack's voice lilted hopefully.

I held up a hand. "Not quite yet. Let me go get a change of clothes and take a quick shower. I'm pretty grungy."

"Yeah, we'd noticed." He ducked as I took a pretend swat at him.

The hot water felt wonderful as I lathered up and washed the grime and sweat away. While I showered, I kept expecting Doris to pop in to invade my privacy or scare me, but she didn't. Her absence made me feel lonely. I hurriedly dressed and rejoined the others at the trestle table.

"Did someone mention making cookies?" I asked.

"Sugar cookies to start, I think," Gillian said. We can let them cool before frosting while we're baking the rest."

We got started and baked a double batch, setting them on cooling racks all over the house. I expected Thor to be curious and inspect them, but he still slept on the couch. I worried about him and Doris. He'd never been so motionless this long before. I stood over his inert form, watching him breathe, reassuring myself that he was alive.

"How about gingerbread next?" Gillian asked, obviously trying to distract me.

I looked up. "I'll pull out the cookie cutters for the

gingerbread men."

After the gingerbread, we took a break and sat around in the living room. It felt good not to have to worry about Mina's being murdered or Marc's being incarcerated. Now, if only... I looked over at Thor, still sleeping on the couch. It'd been hours.

"What else are we making?" Gillian tapped my arm.

"Gumdrop bars," Jack suggested.

"I already have the dough chilling."

"Cool."

By the time the gumdrop bars were in the oven and we were decorating the gingerbread men, I'd started to relax and was humming, "It's Beginning to Look a Lot Like Christmas."

Gillian poured a bag of potpourri into a holly and ivy bowl in the center of the dining room table and lit the candles on either side, filling the room with pine scent. Jack carried wrapping paper, tape, scissors, and labels in from the second bedroom.

"I'll go first." He went back for two bags, set them on the table, and pulled out the first box. "Don't look."

"We won't," Gillian and I called from the kitchen.

In turn, we wrapped our presents and set them under the tree, creating a pile of green, gold, and red cubes like the houses on a village hill with the smaller packages forming hedgerows and bushes around them. I included small presents for Mina, Maya, Theda, and Marc to thank them for all their help. In the morning, we would put together boxes of cookies for some friends, including Ricardo and Mia.

When we were all through, we gathered around the fire to relax.

"I'm really worried about Doris. It's not like her to be gone so long." I put my feet up on the hassock.

Gillian stared into the fire. "She's probably having trouble finding a cooperative squirrel."

"I suppose you're right. We should make an early night of it. Maybe I'll dream of her."

"You miss her." Gillian smiled.

"I do. She's my friend."

"She's a ghost," Jack said.

"That's it. Cutting you off from the beer."

"*What*?" he squawked.

"Kidding. But I am serious about going to bed. I'm exhausted."

"Night," Gillian said from the couch as I rose. "We'll lock up."

Chapter 16

I slept soundly, and when I woke, I lay there for a bit, getting my bearings and going over the events of the previous day. I remembered that Doris was missing, and a deep sadness fell over me. But I pushed myself to get up and dress in a warm Fair Isle sweater and black cords. It was Christmas Eve day, I needed to go to the police station, and I had guests to feed.

Following my nose led me into the kitchen, where Gillian was pulling a pan of cinnamon rolls out of the oven.

"I thought you shouldn't have to worry about breakfast today. Jack and I are following the instructions you left behind. You should relax."

"Thanks. Any sign of Doris?"

"I'm sorry. Not yet. Sit. I'll get a cup of coffee for you."

I glanced over at the sleeping black furry form on the couch. "He's still in the same position."

Gillian poured the coffee and set it in front of me.

"Did you invite George for dinner today?" I asked.

Gillian nodded. "He accepted. You might want to check over the ingredients. I hope I got everything right."

"I am sure you did." I sipped my coffee for a few minutes before I heard the shower shut off.

"Jack's through," Gillian said. "You can use the

bathroom if you need to. I'll feed him and then take my shower."

"I'm fine, and I plan to finish this roll and cup of coffee before I do anything else. These are delicious." I pulled apart the outer spiral of the roll and savored the soft, sweet, frosted center, letting myself enjoy the moment and allowing my sad thoughts to hang, unexamined for the moment.

Jack came out of the bathroom barefoot in jeans and a tee, toweling his hair dry. I scooched over, and he sat next to me at the table.

Gillian ticked down a list. "You helped solve the mysteries in the diary. You helped prove Mina and Marc innocent. You helped catch the killer. You got the video footage for the tour. You planned our Christmas holiday together."

I smiled at her. "Thanks for trying to make me feel better, Gillian. But I won't rest easy until Doris is back and Thor is his normal, obstreperous self again. I'd also really like answers to the Sylvan mystery."

She sat down with the pad containing my notes. "While I'm on a roll, let's look at the next item on your list. Ingredients for Eight Treasures Duck. Are you sure you don't want to do a turkey? From looking at this recipe, I think a turkey would be much easier."

I shook my head. "This is basically the Chinese version of a stuffed turkey, and it's for George. This is what he grew up with in Hawaii. Don't worry. I'll fix it."

"Diced chicken breast, smoked ham, peeled shrimp, fresh chestnuts, bamboo shoots, dried scallops, shitake mushrooms stir-fried with slightly undercooked rice, soy sauce, ginger, scallions, sesame oil, sugar, and rice wine."

As she read, I pulled ingredients out of the pantry. "We're all set. That's everything but the duck."

"Do you baste it like turkey?"

"Using dark soy sauce." I pushed the bottle toward her. "I bought the low sodium version." I sighed and got up. "I'm going to make that statement at the station. I need to get it out of the way. I'll pick up the duck on my way back. I'll feel better with those two tasks completed."

"Drive safely."

I slipped on my jacket and a warm scarf and stepped outside. The air was clear, and the salt scent wafted in on a light breeze. The gentle waves were topped with sea spray that caught the sun like glittering diamonds. The scraggly grass, stiff with cold, scrunched under my boots.

When I got to the station, it was half empty. George came out to get me, looking as though it was an ordinary workday and not Christmas Eve.

I followed him back to his desk. "Hey, you're still coming over for dinner, right?"

"As soon as I finish work."

His desk was covered in paper that seemed to me to be randomly scattered over the surface. Laptop, desk lamp, mug of coffee, and a cruller with chocolate frosting added some color.

"Have a seat."

The room decorations were standard wreaths and holiday-themed stick-ups. A table at one side held plates of cookies and the source of his cruller.

I perused the forms he was filling out. "Did you volunteer to work today?"

He nodded, leaning back in his chair. "Better to let the guys with families have the time off."

"Don't forget tomorrow, too. You don't have to stay long, but I have something for you, and it's my tradition to give presents on Christmas Day."

"I have something for you, too. To respect *your* tradition, I'll bring it over then."

That surprised me. "When did you have time to shop?"

"This is something I've had for a bit. You'll see."

"George, I have some questions—"

"This isn't the time or place. I can take you back to a room."

He handed me the form. I shook my head, tears welling up again. I pick up a pen from his desk and sat opposite him while I wrote, thankful that he didn't send me away.

The statement didn't take long. I wasn't in the mood to embellish. I handed him the form and left.

I headed over to the butcher to pick up the duck. I must have been his last customer of the day because he shut and locked the door behind me. I headed home in a bleak mood matched by a white sky becoming increasingly overcast.

Back at my house, I set the duck on the kitchen counter and returned to the living room to hang up my jacket and check on Thor. Then I started the prep while Gillian set the table and folded the napkins into roses. She used my Christmas tree dishes. Maybe it was silly to have a set of good china I only used at Christmas, but I'd been collecting them since college when I'd found a stack of dessert plates at a thrift shop.

There was a knock at the door. Gillian let Marc in.

"Hi. I wanted to drop this off so that you could have a look when you get a chance. Haven't done post-production finishing touches yet or the voiceovers, but I have all the shots in the order we discussed in the best versions. Don't be concerned with glitches, color matching, etcetera. I can fix a lot later, but I don't want to do more until we know we have a version that you, Ricardo, and Mia like." He handed me a DVD and a flash drive. "You don't need to return this. It's only for your viewing pleasure."

"Thanks. I have some presents for you, Theda, and Maya. Can you come by tomorrow, or do you want them now? I usually don't give out presents until Christmas Day."

"That works for me. I hate to admit this, but better you should hold onto it until tomorrow. I have a really bad habit that comes from living alone." Marc grimaced. "I open presents as soon as I get them."

I laughed, and it felt good. "No problem. I do want to help you break that bad habit. I'll hang on to it until you come by."

He grinned lopsidedly. "My pleasure."

Then he gazed down at his feet and seemed a bit embarrassed. He looked up at me, more serious now.

"I really appreciate what you did for me. Getting the lawyer and setting up a funding page to pay for it. You don't really know me. You went above and beyond."

"You're welcome. I haven't known you long, but I consider you a friend. You came through in a pinch, too. Someone else might have walked away when things got dicey. In fact, if you'd backed out earlier, you wouldn't even have been accused of murder. You were only hired to film, but you stuck it out until the end. I appreciate that."

"I look at it as a new experience I can use when I'm getting into character."

"Glad to be of assistance. See you tomorrow."

I hadn't known him long, but as I watched him walk up the road, I thought Maya was a very lucky woman.

When I joined Gillian in the kitchen, she was wiping down the countertops and the table. "How long does this take? When does it go in the oven?"

"We're starting now. This is my first crack at this. I don't want it to be my last. I've got a couple of hours to marinate the duck while we get everything else done." I unwrapped the bird.

Jack sauntered in. "Anything I can do to help?"

"Not with the cooking," Gillian said. "But you can help to make the place merry and *bright*. You can polish all the old brasswork in the cottage while we chop veggies."

"I can do that. I even know where Cass keeps the rags and brass polish."

Gillian placed her hands on her hips. "Well, look at you! Do you know where the cleaning stuff is in our apartment?"

"If I do, does that mean I have to clean?"

I chuckled. "Nice try, Gillian. You're better off handing him the toilet brush and squirting the blue stuff yourself."

She snorted and pulled the vegetables out of the crisper.

I prepared the marinade of wine, soy sauce, and a dash of sugar. Then cleaned the duck, put it in the mix, and set the timer for 30 minutes. I washed my hands and opened the canned ingredients. Then I cleaned again and began work on the treasures.

If ever there was a time for Doris to appear to harass me, this was it. Yet nothing. I would be alone after Christmas when Jack and Gillian left. Sadness descended, and I sat heavily.

"We're almost ready."

Her tone roused me. "Sorry, Gillian. I'm worried about Doris. I'll miss her if she's gone."

Gillian set her knife down to come over and massage my neck and shoulders. "No moaning over lost ghosts. It's Christmas. There's a Dickens story in there somewhere."

She pulled out her phone, paired it with my speaker, and played Christmas carols.

"Sing along to your heart's content. You can't be down while singing carols." She sang along with "Deck the Halls."

We sang while I fixed the appetizers, Gillian cleaned up the mess, and the duck cooked merrily in the oven.

"When is George due?" Gillian threw the towels in the washing machine, poured two glasses of wine, and handed me one.

"Soon. Since he hasn't called, I'm assuming he can get away on time."

"Good. We don't want the eight treasures ruined after all this work. That is truly amazing stuffing!"

We sat down with Jack and enjoyed our wine until there was a knock at the door. Jack got up to let George in and took the bottle he proffered.

I called from the couch. "Hey, George. I hope

you're hungry."

He sniffed the air and raised his eyebrows. "That's a familiar aroma."

"I am so glad you said that. I really hope it tastes the way it smells."

"I'm sure it will." He hung up his coat and followed Jack into the kitchen, where he opened the oven and drew in a deep breath. "Ah! I can't believe you did this."

"I hope it lives up to your expectations."

"I had no expectation that you would even try this. Thank you for doing it. Brings me a bit of home. I'm grateful."

Jack broke the mood. "Aw, shucks." He looked at the bottle George had handed him. "Nice! Want some of this whiskey?"

"If you're going to open it now, a splash over a rock wouldn't go amiss."

"While you're at it, Jack, could you bring the appetizers out here?"

George followed him out to the living room as he carried the appetizers to the coffee table.

"Keep an eye out for Thor." I said it more out of habit than any idea that he'd be up and around. He would need food and water soon. Maybe even a vet.

Jack gazed around. "Funny, but I haven't seen him all day. Is he in the house? It's really cold out there."

Then I realized that he was no longer sleeping on the couch. I got up to check for myself. He was gone.

"Jack, will you look for him, please? Now I'm worried that he got out, although I'd be really happy if he could muster that much energy. I was afraid he was in a coma."

Jack went down the hall to check the bedrooms, then upstairs to the attic, and returned a few minutes later. "He's asleep up on your bed. I stuck my face in his soft belly fur, and he barely noticed. That's not like him. I think he may be sick or something."

"It's Christmas Eve," I said. "I'm not sure a vet would be available."

The timer dinged. I went into the kitchen and opened the oven. The duck looked perfect, but I barely breathed until we got everything on the table, served the food, and George tasted his first bite. I sucked in a deep breath and exhaled after he closed his eyes and smiled as he savored it.

It seemed redundant, but I asked, anyway. "How is it?"

He opened his eyes. "Perfect. Absolutely perfect. I haven't had this in forever. It might even be better than I remember it."

"That's high praise coming from you."

A thrill of happiness gushed through my body.

"It is indeed." He continued to eat his portion with relish.

"On that recommendation..." Jack served himself and dug in.

I waited until they'd all tried it. Gillian smiled and nodded at me. I helped myself. It was remarkably good. I understood why this was such a special dish. Admittedly, it had taken a lot of work, but it was yummy. I hadn't realized how tense I was until my shoulders relaxed.

Gillian paused with her fork midway to her mouth. "It really is good. I'm glad you talked me out of turkey."

"It's always good to experiment." I sipped my wine.

Jack said, "Even when it ends in disaster. I tried microwaving my oatmeal one morning to save time. *Blooshh!*" He made an explosive gesture with both hands. "All over the inside of the microwave. Milk and oats everywhere."

Gillian cracked up. "I made him clean it."

"Epic fail." Jack helped himself to seconds.

"George, I don't want to spoil the mood, but please, after all we've been through, will you answer a few questions?"

He finished his wine and set the glass down. "What do you want to know?"

"The woman in red who showed up at the end, is she indeed Sylvan Woodbright as she claimed?"

"Yes, though she hasn't been Sylvan Woodbright for many years. I'm sure more details will come out at the trial, but she and Liberty Byrne are mother and daughter."

"So, Libby couldn't track the name change."

"Looks like Sylvan changed her name several times and not necessarily through the courts. As a cop, I think it makes her look guilty of something. She never renewed her American passport, but she said she never officially gave up her citizenship. However, someone had her declared dead, and that has thrown her status into doubt." He chuckled. "It's not really funny, but she had a bit of trouble getting into the country—not only because of being officially dead but also because of heightened security—but her husband is a diplomat and has a lot of pull. I'm sure they'll get it sorted out. She traveled on an Egyptian passport."

"What did she say about abandoning Libby?"

"She denied abandoning her. She said she was too immature to be a good mother to her, so gave her up for adoption for her own good. But the hospital had Sylvan's real name, and that's where the name game started. While there, she'd met an older man, a Filipino of Spanish descent. He took her in, and eventually, she married him and took his name. She says she was faithful to him, and they traveled all over Asia. Eventually, she inherited his estate at his death.

"On a trip to Hong Kong, she met her current husband, an Egyptian diplomat, and changed her identity again. She is well and truly in love with him and says she has been completely honest with him. He was delighted to find out she had a daughter and tracked her down. They paid anonymously for Libby's education. When Sylvan saw the coded announcement of the reunion, they made the trip here—with the delays I mentioned—intending to contact her daughter."

"He knows everything about her?"

George nodded. "So she says. They have no children of their own, so he wants to adopt Libby and make her his heir."

"But she's going to prison!"

"Not if they can help it. Did I mention their connections? They're completely reframing the narrative. It seems your murderous professor might indeed get off. They're working the angle that she was having a breakdown from all the trauma in her life and reliving her nightmares. Also, they're claiming that one murder was an accident, another was self-defense, and that Alcott had a heart attack."

"She may not be an American citizen, and her

husband is a diplomat. Does that complicate prosecution?"

"It needs to be untangled. Sylvan is quite wealthy now and has hired some very prestigious lawyers for her daughter. The information we're getting is mostly from lawyers in the service of getting her daughter off on the murder charges."

"Excuse me?"

"You heard me. As I said, they're claiming the first was an accident. Mirabella fell on the equipment, tripping Libby, who fell on top of her, innocently causing her injury. You should be hearing that story on the news. Sylvan is doing press conferences, highlighting her daughter's childhood trauma."

"How do they account for the other two murders?" Jack asked. "You said self-defense and heart attack."

"But the autopsy?" I said. "Didn't that prove poisoning?"

He shrugged. "They want their experts to examine all the bodies and run their tests. It's going to be a media circus for a while."

"But there were a lot of witnesses to an attempted murder down in the steam tunnels. How are they going to get around that?"

"We'll have to wait for the trial."

"Was Libby the one shedding skin flakes?"

He nodded. "She was. Libby has psoriasis, and the DNA from her scales matches that on two of the victims. We also found flakes at the scene of the attack on her, which led us to believe that the killer had psoriasis. Marc gave us a DNA sample, and there was no match, so we let him go if you remember."

"Any idea why Libby was so sure that the club

members had done something to her mother?" I asked.

George shook his head. "We do know that, because Sylvan gave her real name, Libby was raised by relatives in Wisconsin, got her bachelor's degree there. Her Ph.D. is from Berkeley. She wasn't destitute, nor was she alone in the world. Although the relatives didn't think much of her or her mother, they happily took the money Sylvan sent."

"Wait. Who declared her dead?"

"The relatives."

"But they knew she wasn't. They could have told Libby at any time."

"Until fairly recently, I think it suited everyone to keep Libby in the dark," George said. "When we mentioned the relatives, Sylvan started hedging her answers, and it all gets a little murky once the lawyers got involved, but I gather it had something to do with her first husband being Catholic. Her timing was way off."

"Are they getting along? Talking?"

"Thick as thieves; you should pardon the expression."

****

The next day was Christmas. When I woke, I grabbed my robe and slippers and ran downstairs, holding the railing to avoid falling ass over teakettle in my hurry.

I smelled coffee and joined Gillian in the kitchen. I took the cup she offered and sipped, letting the caffeinated warmth heat me from the inside out. "Where is my brother? We've got presents to open!"

Jack emerged from the bathroom. His hair couldn't seem to make up its mind which direction it was going.

"Don't get your knickers in a twist. I'm coming."

Gillian plated a cinnamon coffee cake and set it on the coffee table. I grabbed my cup and hers and carried them out. Then I went back for plates and forks. Jack plopped down on one end of the couch. I set a plate in front of each of us.

"Hey, youngest. You get to pass out the gifts. Don't get comfortable."

"Food and coffee first. We're not children anymore," Jack said.

"Could have fooled me," I said.

"Besides, technically, Gillian's the youngest. She's also the most wide awake. You wouldn't want me to give you the wrong presents now, would you?" He smirked.

Gillian rolled her eyes but went over to the tree, picked up several gifts, and read the tags. She tucked one back under the tree. "I see George is getting his presents at your house."

"It's from me, and he's coming back today."

She handed me one. "This is from us, and it's really for Thor."

I ripped the shiny green paper from the cylinder, and it flattened out into a square. "It's beautiful! Did you make this?"

"Jack did. He hand-hooked the whole thing. We thought Thor might like to sleep on it. He seems to like rugs."

"True. He's always asleep on the hearth-rug when he's down here. Thanks, guys." I laid it on the floor for him. "The rectangular box is from me to you, Gillian."

She picked up the box and untied the silver ribbon carefully.

"Hey! What about me?" Jack said.

Gillian shrugged. "You wanted me to pass out the presents." But she relented and tossed him a large plaid-wrapped package.

Jack ripped off the paper and held up a burgundy velour robe.

"Thanks, hon." He kissed her.

"Glad you like it."

The doorbell rang.

"I'll get it," he said.

Mina followed Jack into the living room. "I hope I'm not interrupting."

Jack took her packages as Gillian helped her off with her long coat and scarf.

I eyed the plastic container that wasn't wrapped. "Hi, Mina. Would you like some tea and coffee cake?"

She shook her head. "No, thank you. I've eaten. I wanted to bring over a few small things to thank you for all your help and because it's that time of year." She took the packages from Jack. "I made a batch of lemon bars, so these are for you, Cass. I know how much you like them." She handed me the plastic container.

"Thank you so much, Mina. I will definitely enjoy these."

She smiled and handed a slim box to Gillian and an envelope to Jack. "I hope you like these."

Gillian set the box I'd given her down and carefully unwrapped Mina's gift. "Oh!" She held up a gauzy scarf in the delicate blues and grays of the ocean and sky at twilight. "This is gorgeous." She wrapped it around her neck. "I love it."

Jack slit open his envelope and laughed. "Perfect."

"They're friends of mine. I thought you'd like a

tour of the distillery and a tasting."

"Absolutely!" He tapped the gift card. "This is perfect. Thanks."

Mina bowed slightly. "You're welcome."

"We have a present for you." I bent down to select a present from under the tree. "This is from all of us."

Mina opened it and withdrew a forest green, leather-bound diary with a world tree on the cover and her name embossed in gold. She stroked it with her fingertips. "This is lovely. Thank you all." She glanced down at Gillian's discarded present. "I see I've interrupted your gift exchange."

"That's all right. We were hoping to see you today. You don't have to go," I said.

She shook her head. "I have other rounds to make but thank you." She slipped back into her coat. "Have a *Joyous Noël*."

After she left, I cleared my throat and glanced meaningfully at my present to Gillian that lay forgotten at her feet.

"Oh, sorry." She picked it up and finished opening it. "It's lovely, and it goes with the scarf." Gillian held up a blue sapphire necklace.

"I bought it at Crystalline. Samantha said she thought you'd like it."

"I do." She fastened it around her neck.

Jack tossed her a very small present. "Open this one next."

She raised an eyebrow but did as he asked. Laughing, she put a sapphire cocktail ring on her finger. "I sense a conspiracy."

Jack kissed and hugged her. "You'd be right. I know you've put up with a lot from me lately."

"I don't know how I deal with you." Her giggle was smothered by his kiss. Reluctantly, she pushed away from him. "Later."

"Anything you say, sweet pea." He let her go and went to poke around under the tree. "Ah, here it is." He handed it to Gillian and took one for himself.

Gillian passed the package wrapped in gold to me. "Hope you like it."

I ripped the paper and opened the lid of the box. "It's beautiful." I held up the charm bracelet. "A black enameled cat, a crescent moon on a blue enameled circle, a silver circle that says 'She persisted,' my name in another silver circle, a clamshell, a jack o' lantern, and a Christmas tree."

"The crescent moon and 'She persisted' are from Mina. She ran into me while I was buying it and wanted to contribute."

"I'll have to thank her for it when I return her container. This is really thoughtful, Gillian. I love it." I sat down and had another square of coffee cake.

"More coffee?"

"Yes, please."

The doorbell rang again.

Gillian detoured to the door to let George in.

Gesturing toward the tree, I said, "Join the group."

George took his jacket off and handed me a box that was a bit too large to be a ring, but hey, I never sneeze at jewelry of any kind.

"Thanks. Gee, I didn't get you anything." I walked over to the tree. "Oh, yes, I guess I did." I picked up a somewhat larger package and gave it to him. "Little bit of trepidation here. I'm not sure what you'll think."

"Let's open them together."

George ripped the paper off, revealing a slender book. He ran his finger over the gold embossed title *Journey* and his name on the cover. Then he opened it and sat down abruptly as if his legs had gone limp under him.

I watched him, my package half-opened in my hands, as he silently flipped through the pages, emotions playing across his expressive face. I'd spent hours looking through my photos and reminiscing.

We'd gone to Hawaii when we were in college. I'd included some of those vacation photos not only to remind him of his family and home but also to help him remember how great I looked in a bathing suit. There were pictures of our study dates, too. I debated adding the photo of me lying on my stomach on the old green couch in my apartment with my knees bent and my feet in the air. I supported my chin on my hands and had a single rose in my teeth. I could tell when he hit that one. He laughed and looked up at me, his eyes crinkling. But the book was mostly about his adventures and exploits: scuba diving, surfing, tennis.

He closed the book. The tears in his eyes took my breath away. My fingers froze.

He set the book down and took the box from me. Then opened it and removed the diamond teardrop necklace. I lifted my hair as he fastened it around my neck.

He wrapped me in his arms and kissed me. I forgot where I was until I heard Jack and Gillian clapping.

George released me and took a little bow. He turned to me. "Do you like it?"

I touched the necklace. "I love it."

He took a deep breath. "Thank you for the memory

book. I don't think I've seen some of those pictures before."

I smiled. "Good times." I had a sudden memory of Doris. "I wish…"

Doris flickered and solidified on the circular stairs behind George. She wore her favorite flapper outfit, including the feather in her headband.

"Miss me?"

A word about the author...

Rena Leith lives ten minutes from either the Atlantic Ocean or the Delaware Bay with two Maine Coons who get pushy from time to time. Her Cass Peake cozy mystery series consists of three books so far: *Murder Beach*, *Coastal Corpse*, and *A Corpse for Christmas*. She's also written a romantic novella entitled *The Great Christmas Jelly Cookie Hunt*.

She belongs to the Jersey Shore Writers, whose anthology includes her short story "A Fish Tale." Like most writers, she's traveled extensively and worked at many different and weird jobs. As she says, "It's all grist for the mill."

https://www.renaleith.com

If you enjoyed this story, leaving a review at your favorite book retailer or reader website would be much appreciated. Thank you!